BORGAZ
HOW THE ALIENS WERE WON

HONEY PHILLIPS

Copyright © 2023 by Honey Phillips

All rights reserved. No part of this book may be used or reproduced by any means, graphic, electronic, or mechanical, including photocopying, recording, taping or by any information storage retrieval system without the written permission of the author.

Disclaimer

This book is a work of fiction. Names, characters, places, and incidents are products of the author's imagination or are used fictitiously and are not to be construed as real. Any resemblance to actual events, locales, organizations, or people, living or dead, is entirely coincidental.

Cover Design by Mariah Sinclair
Edited by Lindsay York at LY Publishing Services

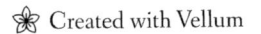

❀ Created with Vellum

CHAPTER 1

Mary pulled the letter out of her pocket for what felt like the hundredth time. The battered note had taken almost four months to follow her through five different locations, from the modest house her parents had rented when they first arrived in Port Cantor to her current minuscule room with the stained carpet and the walls that shook each time a ship departed from the nearby spaceport. The housing near the spaceport was little more than hastily assembled prefabs intended for passing crewmen, but it was the only thing she could afford.

She'd had such high hopes when they first moved to the city. Even though her parents had been forced to sell their farm in the face of the neighboring landowner's increasingly open threats, she'd been optimistic about the future. Unfortunately, she hadn't been prepared for the realities of life in the city. Even that first house in a nice neighborhood had been a shock with the neighbors right outside her window, and the constant hum of traffic, and the stars blocked by the lights of the city.

The adjustment had been a struggle, and then her parents died in a freak maglev train accident and her whole world had come crashing down around her. Due to her naivety, it hadn't taken long for the credits to run out, along with any chance of finishing the education they'd tried to provide for her. She had regretted that, but even worse, it left her with few resources when looking for a job.

She'd been brought up on a farm; she knew how to milk a cow, not program a replicator. She also had an unfortunate habit of speaking her mind when encountering stupidity. As a result jobs were hard to find and easy to lose—as she'd realized yet again two days ago. Her former boss had not taken kindly to her rejection of his advances, nor her blunt suggestion as to what he could do with the pathetic little dick he'd had the nerve to brandish at her. Righteous indignation had carried her off with her head high, but it hadn't taken long for despair to follow.

The letter had arrived the same day. Smoothing it out, she read through it once again.

Dear Mary,

It seems like such a long time since I've seen you! I hope you and your parents are doing well.

I have some very exciting news—I'm married! To an alien, of all things. His name is Harkan, and he's big and strong and protective—a little too protective sometimes!—and I'm happier than I ever thought I could be. I hope you will get to meet him—which brings me to my second piece of news.

Do you remember that mysterious group of aliens that took over the old Wainwright ranch? After you were gone they started showing up in town, and now all of them are married too! Harkan was on his way to ask them for help when he ended up in my barn. To make a long story short, not only did they help him, they "encouraged" Matthew Johnson to sell Harkan all the property he had acquired!

Harkan is planning to use the property as a way for former soldiers to find peace and healing through working on the land and taking over the old farms. I think it's a wonderful idea, but I know you and your family didn't want to leave. We've agreed that if you want to return, we'll sign your farm back over to you. I understand you've probably moved on with your exciting new life in the city, but we wanted to make the offer.

Please let me know what you think. Even if you don't want to come back, I hope we will meet again one day. I still miss you!

Love,

Rosie

Rosie—married to an alien. The old Mary would have been shocked, but there were so many aliens in the city, especially around the spaceport, that the idea didn't seem as farfetched as it would have once. How the two of them had speculated about the mysterious males who had bought the ranch back then, full of girlish dreams—and no real idea of life outside the farm.

Her mouth twisted. She was a long way from the naive girl she'd been. Was it even possible to go back home again? *Home.* Even after all this time, the farm still felt like home. But despite the happy memories, she also remembered how hard they had worked. Could she do it on her own? The few credits she'd managed to save might pay for the trip back, especially if she could also barter some work as well, but they wouldn't be enough to raise the stake she'd need to get started. Unless...

Also for the hundredth time, she pulled out her mother's necklace. Her grandmother had brought it from Earth when she first arrived as a colonist, and it was the only thing of value she owned. She'd held on to it all this time, but for what? Wouldn't rebuilding the farm be a far better tribute to her family than a piece of jewelry?

The rumble of a departing ship vibrated through the walls, and she moved to the tiny window to catch a glimpse of it soaring into the sky. Some might have seen the ship as a symbol of freedom, but all it did was make her long for home. *Home,* she thought again, picturing the small white house nestled in a grove of trees and surrounded by rolling green hills. Yes. It was time to go home.

"Sorry, Mama," she whispered as she carefully placed the necklace back in its box. "I hope you'd understand."

SIX WEEKS LATER, MARY WALKED DOWN THE DUSTY ROAD towards her farm. She could have waited another day and ridden out with the wagonload of supplies she'd purchased from Mr. Armstrong, the shopkeeper in Wainwright, but she'd been too impatient to wait.

S'kal, the big, green alien who was the wagon master of the caravan she had traveled with, had also offered to escort her to her home but she'd turned him down as well. Despite his intimidating appearance and gruff manner, he was nice enough— agreeing to let her work off some of her passage and making sure no one bothered her—but she needed to do this on her own.

The fields flanking the roads were just beginning to show the signs of spring, a faint haze of green covering the winter brown. The air was still brisk but the sun was shining, and she felt her spirits lifting as she walked, glad of the exercise after the long weeks riding in the caravan. Her long skirt created little swirls of dust around her feet, but she was glad she'd changed into it before reaching Wainwright. Traditional clothing still predominated in the town, although she'd noticed several women wearing pants. Change might be coming to Wainwright, but it wasn't coming quickly.

The road diverged ahead, one way leading to Rosie's farm and the other to hers. She hesitated for a moment, then took the branch that would lead her home, walking alongside the creek and then up over a small rise to the grove that sheltered her family's house. Her steps quickened as she came around the final curve before coming to an abrupt halt.

"Damn you, Matthew Johnson. Damn you to hell."

The neighboring landowner had been so eager to acquire their land that he'd forced her parents to sell, but for what? He'd clearly had no interest in using or even maintaining the property. The fields surrounding the house were little more than weeds surrounded by broken fences, and the barn looked crooked. The small white house she'd loved was barely recognizable—paint peeling from the siding, the porch roof leaning crookedly to one side, and broken panes in the arched gable window of her old bedroom.

The amount of work it would take to restore the farm to its former condition suddenly overwhelmed her, and her knees threatened to give way. She sank down on the brittle grass next to the road as she took in the rundown remnants of the once thriving farm. Had she made a dreadful mistake in coming back?

Her head dropped to her knees as she sat there, fighting back the tears, but eventually the surrounding quiet seeped into her. There were no spaceships taking off, no strange voices yelling in strange languages. The only sound was a small purple bird—one of Cresca's few native lifeforms—tweeting in a nearby tree. She took a deep breath and stood, dusting off her skirts.

It might be more work than she'd anticipated, and it might take longer to make the farm profitable, but she wasn't going to give up now. Perhaps it wasn't even as bad as it looked from here. Picking up her pack, she marched determinedly down the road.

CHAPTER 2

*B*orgaz did his best to look attentive as Temel, his friend and former commander, laid out his plans for their new property. Personally he thought the whole idea was absurd—what place did warriors have on a farm, let alone in an isolated community far from any real civilization? Then again, there hadn't been a place for them on the mining planet where they'd worked security or in the spaceport here on Cresca either.

Seven years since the war had ended and every day still felt like a struggle. Each night the familiar nightmares haunted his sleep, leaving him exhausted and bitter, but he had accepted the fact that this was his life now. If he chose to compensate with one too many drinks and more than one too many fights, what difference did it make to anyone?

Anyone except Temel, that is. Or perhaps Temel and his fellow warriors. Naffon, trying to juggle three of the round fruits the humans called apples, his big grin hiding the self-destructive streak that led into ever more dangerous mischief. Kalpar, leaning against the counter with his usual expression of bored cynicism, growing colder with each passing year. And Temel, the leader they would all die for, trying to mask his worries behind his detailed plans for this mad venture.

"Is that clear?" Temel asked.

"Is it clear that you expect us to perform manual labor for the uncertain promise of a crop that could be destroyed by drought or floods or insects and might not actually return a profit?" Kalpar drawled. "Unfortunately, yes."

Temel rubbed the frown lines that seemed permanently embedded between his horns.

"You agreed to come, Kalpar."

"Also unfortunately."

Borgaz bristled, but before he could challenge the other male, Kalpar straightened and headed for the door, pausing long enough to drop his hand on Temel's shoulder.

"So I will begin by making myself acquainted with these animals we have acquired." Kalpar reached out and grabbed one of Naffon's apples. "Come along, youngster. Perhaps those charms you're always bragging about will work on animals— they certainly don't work on females."

"You're just jealous because you don't have any charm—or any females."

Naffon grinned as he caught the remaining apples and stuffed them in his pockets, but Borgaz saw the shadow cross Kalpar's face before he drew one of his hidden knives and flicked it across the room. The knife landed with a solid *thunk* in the wooden counter next to Naffon, but his grin only broadened, his expression challenging.

"Or maybe you're just too old to be interested?"

"Enough," Temel said tiredly as Kalpar reached for his other sleeve. "Thank you for checking on the animals, Kalpar. I've downloaded a schedule of their requirements to everyone's datapad. Naffon, go check the feed inventory."

Naffon started to salute, then nodded instead and left. Kalpar retrieved his knife and followed, pausing at the door to look back.

"Don't worry. I have no intention of letting him provoke me."

Temel nodded. "I know."

A rare smile crossed Kalpar's face.

"But that doesn't mean I won't be happy to introduce him to the joys of manure spreading."

As Kalpar left, Temel sighed and sat back in his chair.

"I'm not going to ask you if you think this is a bad idea because you've already made your feelings known, but do you at least see why I think it's necessary to try?"

"Because we're all fucked up in our own ways?" he asked dryly, then shrugged. "I agree with that part."

"Artek said that hard work and natural surroundings really helped his warriors."

He shrugged again.

"I know he's a friend of yours, so perhaps it did. That doesn't mean it's the cure for any of us." Or that there was a cure for the damage the war had caused. "But I'm here, aren't I?"

"You are." Temel finally smiled. "Which means it's time to put you to work. Harkan provided this map of the original fourteen farms. From what he said, this plot and the surrounding four were all actively farmed by the previous owner. I'd like you to inspect the rest and see what infrastructure remains. Are there any useful buildings or usable assets?"

Harkan was a Riasi, also a former warrior, and owned all of the property they now inhabited. He and his mate worked the closest farm but they intended to make the remaining farms available to other former warriors as long as they would commit to working the land for a minimum of five years. Because Harkan was busy with his own farm and his pregnant mate, he'd been happy to place the project in Temel's hands.

"Do you really think any of us will end up on one of the smaller farms?" he asked.

The prospect horrified him—to be completely alone with his memories and his nightmares? He barely suppressed a shudder.

Temel shrugged. "Perhaps. Or perhaps we will simply make them ready for others. There is room enough for all of us to be here together—and room enough to be apart."

His friend was quite correct. The house had been built by the former owner as an expression of his wealth and while it was far less grand than some of the homes on Borgaz's home planet of Erythra, it was a sizable residence by Cresca standards.

"Apart is definitely preferable if Naffon is going to keep provoking Kalpar," he muttered, and Temel sighed.

"Which is why I'm sending you on an inspection tour."

"Understood. I'll report back tonight, or perhaps tomorrow," he added.

While he didn't want to be on his own permanently, a period alone would be welcome. The decision to move to the property and all of the necessary details had consumed most of his time for the past few months.

"Very well. Just take a comm with you."

"Yes, matma."

Temel shook his head but grinned at the familiar nickname. A matma was an avian with a habit of herding her nestlings into a circle, clucking anxiously until they were all accounted for.

"Go on with you before I start pulling *my* knives."

Borgaz laughed, saluted, and left. He could hear Naffon protesting loudly from the barn where the milking animals were kept, but he avoided the structure and went to the paddock instead. The animals the humans called horses were a genetically modified version of animals from their own planet, but they were not dissimilar to zebards, the riding animals from his own planet. He had ridden them in his childhood, and the task of saddling one felt unexpectedly familiar. A short time later, he was on his way, settling easily into the rhythm of his mount as he left the main house behind.

The sun rode high overhead, washing everything in a clear golden light as he started his survey. An unaccustomed sense of peace settled over him as he rode, looking down at the river running through the bottomland. Several small creeks diverged from the river, providing water for the various farms, although in at least one case, the creek had been dammed to cut off the supply of water. He made a note and moved on.

This was not... unpleasant, he decided. He still wasn't convinced that the venture would be successful, or that he would choose to remain even if it were, but perhaps his time here wouldn't be as miserable as he'd feared. Up ahead the road diverged so he chose the way closest to the main farm. He would work his way out over the afternoon and camp at one of the outer farms tonight.

As he crossed over the boundary onto the smaller property, he noticed the many signs of neglect and deferred maintenance. If all of the smaller farms were in this shape, a male would have to be very dedicated to take on the task of restoring one. He came to a halt in front of the farmhouse and after a brief survey decided it was livable, despite its rundown condition. He made another note and was about to move on when he heard a crash from inside the building.

What the fuck? His body immediately went into battle mode, his senses sharpening as he swung silently down from the horse. He tied it behind a bush and approached the house, his hand automatically reaching for the blaster he no longer carried. Despite the lack, a fierce grin crossed his face, already anticipating a battle.

The warped boards of the porch floor barely squeaked as he made his way lightly across them and in through the open front door. A wide hallway led from the front of the house to the back, a stairway rising along one side. Rooms opened to either side of the hall but they were shrouded in shadow, the windows covered with heavy curtains. The light coming in through the doorway illuminated the dust floating in the air as another crash came from behind a closed door at the rear of the house.

Stealthy footsteps carried him to the door, and he paused. His instincts told him to go in hard and fast, overwhelming his enemy, but caution had replaced his impulsiveness many battles ago.

A clatter of what sounded like crockery falling came from behind the door. The kitchen perhaps? Surely no one was foolish enough to think that this dilapidated wreck contained food supplies.

Curiously soft footsteps came towards his position and he waited, his body humming with anticipation as the door swung open.

"Got you," he growled as his arms closed around the intruder, forcing his hands behind his back.

No—*her* hands behind *her* back. Wide, startled eyes stared up at him, their color somewhere between grey and blue, while the deliciously soft, luscious breasts pressed against his chest left no doubt that his captive was female. Neither did the delicate features or the pretty pink lips drawn into a startled *oh* or the sweet scent tantalizing him and urging him to pull her closer.

Mine.

CHAPTER 3

Don't scream.

The warning echoed through Mary's head as she stared up at the huge alien male holding her captive. The amber eyes of a predator glowed in the dimly lit hall and she froze instinctively, too afraid to move. He had red skin and a smooth scalp, the small horns curved up on either side of his head giving him a devilish look. His hand tightened around her wrists, not painful but inescapable as he pulled her a fraction closer to that massive body.

Fear threatened to make her legs tremble, but one of the first lessons she'd learned after her parents' death was never to show that she was afraid.

"Let go of me at once and get the hell off my farm."

Her voice came out surprisingly firm but he didn't seem to hear it, his gaze still focused on her face. Her heart thudded against her ribs so hard she felt sick, but she refused to try and struggle against a grip she had no chance of escaping. Then he grinned, a wicked grin that made her stomach do an odd little flip.

"Such a fierce little female."

He pulled her even closer and, oh God, was that an erection, before he suddenly dropped her hands and stepped back, his smile replaced by a fearsome scowl.

"You are the intruder, female. What are you doing here?"

"I told you—this is my farm." Wasn't it? *I really should have gone to see Rosie first*, she thought, but she refused to show any doubt, glaring back at him. "Rosie told me that she was giving my family farm back to me."

"Rosie? Harkan's mate?"

"Yes." The pieces suddenly came together, and some of her tension disappeared. "Are you one of the soldiers they're trying to help? Because I'm sorry, but this farm isn't available."

His scowl deepened.

"I am a warrior, not a soldier, and I do not require anyone's help. I am only here because my commander requested that I accompany him."

She couldn't help a nervous glance over her shoulder.

"He's here too? Where?"

"He is here on the property, but he did not accompany me on this trip. We are alone."

Was that intended as a threat? Her pulse started to race again as she realized how close they were in the empty house.

"W-why are you here?"

She couldn't prevent the slight tremor in her voice, but although his grim look remained he took another step back, his hands open at his sides.

"I mean you no harm, female," he said gruffly. "I was sent to inspect the individual farms and see what was salvageable. Very little in this case."

Irritation at his dismissive tone made her forget her fear.

"I disagree, but in any case, it's not your concern. You should concentrate on the farms that don't belong to someone."

"You are intending to restore this farm? Do you have a mate?"

There was a curious intensity to the last question but she chose to ignore it, lifting her chin and glaring at him.

"No, I don't. And I don't need one."

Those amber eyes swept down over her body and she blushed, suddenly conscious of her attire—or lack of it. Hot from the long walk, she had stripped off the heavy dress, leaving her in her thin cotton camisole and knee-length drawers. He studied her with what she was sure was appreciation, but then he scowled again.

"You are too small. You cannot do this on your own."

"I can and I will. Now go do your inspection somewhere else. Go on, shoo."

"Shoo?" he repeated, raising an eyebrow.

"Yes. It means leave, depart, go."

He ignored her, looking at the kitchen door.

"What was the crash I heard?"

"It was nothing," she said firmly. "Now, please go."

"You are a poor liar, female."

Without waiting for a response, he pushed open the door and stalked into the kitchen, his tail lashing behind him. *A tail?* Biting back another useless protest, she followed him.

"It looks worse than it is," she muttered as she followed his appalled gaze around the room.

The once neat kitchen was now in a horrendous state. The small vermin native to the planet had obviously found a way into the room, leaving piles of debris scattered across the floor. There was a dark stain beneath the sink from a long, slow leak and the pantry cabinet was now in pieces on the floor along with a pile of broken dishes.

"It looks as if you attempted to open the storage cupboard and pulled it down on top of you." He was scowling again. "You could have been injured."

"That's not what happened." *Exactly.* It had tipped to the side instead of on top of her. "And I'm not hurt, so you see, everything is fine."

"Everything is not fine," he snapped, hauling the cabinet upright with terrifying ease. "This place is not habitable."

She crossed her arms over her chest and glared at him.

"It's perfectly habitable. It simply needs a good scrubbing—which I will do as soon as you leave."

His gaze dropped to her crossed arms, and she realized that the position had caused her breasts to swell over the low neckline of the camisole. She quickly dropped her arms but he'd already looked away, apparently immune to whatever feminine charms she might possess.

"Where is your cleaning equipment? And before you tell me you don't have any, I will point out that you just told me you intended to clean this space."

He waited for an answer, as huge and immobile as a boulder in the middle of her kitchen, and she finally sighed and pointed at the door to the back porch.

"In there. Since you're so determined to play maid, I'm going to go and change into something more appropriate for the lady of the house."

Triumphant at having the last word, she turned to march out of the room.

"On the contrary, I think you look very appropriate."

His rough voice stopped her dead in her tracks.

"W-what did you say?" she stammered, her cheeks heating as she whirled around.

There was definitely no mistaking the appreciation in his gaze this time, and her stomach flipped, but once again the expression disappeared behind a scowl.

"You should change," he said gruffly. "Shoo."

Too unnerved to argue, she turned and fled.

CHAPTER 4

What the hell is wrong with me, Borgaz wondered as he found the broom and began attacking the debris on the kitchen floor. He had made note of the deplorable state of the farm, although it was irrelevant if his female had claimed it. He should move on and complete his assignment. He certainly should not remain here, rendering assistance she clearly did not want and just as clearly needed.

The sense of order that the military had beaten into him was offended by the surrounding chaos, but more than that, he was concerned for her safety. *I will just make sure everything is secure and then I will leave*, he decided as he swept up the last of the broken crockery. A few pieces had escaped the crash and he placed them on the counter to be washed, frowning at the dark stain on the floor. *And perhaps take care of the leak.*

In addition to cleaning supplies, the back porch contained some primitive tools, and it took little time to secure the cabinet to the wall. Some oil applied to the hinges made it easier to open, and he nodded with satisfaction before moving on to the leak. He had his head beneath the sink when she reappeared.

"What do you think you're doing?"

He'd caught the sound of her footsteps and a hint of her deliciously sweet scent so he didn't startle at her approach. Instead, he kept his gaze firmly on his task.

"Repairing your plumbing. These pipes are a disgrace."

"What does a warrior know about plumbing?"

He ignored the skepticism in her voice. He'd turned his hand to many different things over the years.

"Enough to know that this will be a makeshift repair at best. It would be better to replace all of the pipes."

Perhaps there were some additional supplies back at the main house...

"Since I can't afford new pipes, these will have to do. Thank you for looking at them," she added grudgingly. "But I am sure you have other places to go now."

He tightened the last joint and slid out from beneath the sink and found her frowning down at him. Instead of the thin white clothing she'd worn previously, she was now dressed in pants in a heavy blue material that accentuated the luscious curves of her ass and legs. Her shirt was also of heavier cloth, but it was fitted enough to reveal the fullness of her breasts.

The change of clothing had done nothing to lessen her appeal. Even worse, her glorious hair had been restrained into a thick braid that would be perfect for wrapping around his fist as he pulled her down over his cock. His shaft immediately flexed at the image, but he did his best to keep his face composed as he rose to his feet.

"You do realize that this farm will require extensive work to be restored to a viable operation, don't you? I also do not consider this house to be safe."

Her shoulders went back, pushing her breasts up against the confining fabric, and his cock hardened despite his best intentions.

"We occupied this house until we left, and it hasn't been empty that long."

"Occupied perhaps, but not maintained. I do not mean to imply any fault on your part, female. But if this place were properly looked after, you would not have so much work to do to make it livable."

The truth of his statement did not make her any happier. She looked uncertainly around the kitchen for a moment, then lifted her chin.

"Matthew made the last few years… difficult for my family."

Unexpected anger filled him at her comment. Perhaps it was just as well that the previous owner was long gone or he would have been tempted to teach the bastard the consequences of harassing an innocent female and her family.

"But regardless of how it looks," she continued, "This house belongs to me and I intend to live here. So if you'd kindly see yourself out, I'll get back to work."

"You do not have the strength to do it alone."

Her brows drew together, those perfect little lips compressing into a thin line.

"You seem to think you know an awful lot about me. I don't recall asking for your advice—or your help."

"You did not. That does not change the fact that it would be unwise to allow you to stay here."

The words had barely left his mouth before she turned on her heel and left. He watched, slightly bemused, as she stormed out the back door, only to come stomping right back in.

"Allow me? How dare you! My life and my choices are none of your business."

Her whole body radiated fury and indignation, her fists clenched at her sides, and she suddenly reminded him of a fojii —a small animal native to his planet that would puff up its fur to appear larger and more intimidating—and his lips curved in an unwilling smile. Her eyes narrowed.

"Are you laughing at me?"

"Of course not, female."

"And stop calling me female! My name is Mary."

"Mary." He liked the taste of it on his tongue. "I am Borgaz, of House Carnak."

He found himself taking her hand and bowing, some long forgotten lesson in etiquette surfacing as his tail wrapped around their joined hands. Her small fingers trembled in his, and she suddenly looked uncertain rather than angry.

"Borgaz..."

His name had never sounded as sweet before, but he forced himself to focus on the more important subject of her safety. Before he could pursue the conversation, his wrist comm buzzed, the tone indicating a call from Temel. He cursed under his breath as he reluctantly dropped her hand and answered it.

"Yes?"

Temel's image appeared on the small screen.

"How is the survey proceeding?"

"Fine, Commander. There's very little on this part of the property that can be reclaimed," he said, not looking at Mary's stiff figure.

"We expected as much. Did you finish your initial sweep?"

"Not quite yet. I'll complete it tomorrow. There was..." He hesitated.

"There was *what*?" Temel asked sharply.

"Nothing important. I will report back when I'm finished."

Temel did not look convinced, but he nodded.

"Good. I know you did not intend to return until tomorrow, but I would like to hold a meeting tonight with all of us, including Harkan and Rosie. If you can return before then, please do so."

"Very well," he agreed, and ended the communication.

"Why didn't you tell him that I have reclaimed my farm?" Mary demanded. "Is he going to object?"

He could feel her worry in every tense muscle of her small frame, but he ruthlessly suppressed his desire to offer her comfort—and other things.

"Of course not. It simply seemed more appropriate to discuss it in person."

"You mean instead of while I was standing here?"

She crossed her arms over her chest again, and despite the additional clothing it was just as provocative a position.

"Precisely." He hesitated again. "Temel has arranged a meeting for this evening. Perhaps it would be best if you attended as well to present your claim."

"It's not a claim. It's a fact."

"Your friend will be there as well."

Her expression finally softened.

"Rosie? I do want to see her, but..."

She looked around the kitchen again, and he could easily read the thoughts crossing her expressive little face.

"I will help you finish your cleaning so the house is more... suitable when you return."

Although he would do everything he could to persuade her to remain at the main house instead of returning to this decrepit dwelling.

Her chin rose again.

"That's not necessary."

"Would you prefer that I simply remove you from the premises until it has been rendered safe?"

"You wouldn't dare!"

"I most certainly would." He leaned down until his eyes were level with hers. Her lips parted, impossibly tempting, but he needed to make his position clear. "Make no mistake, little fojii,

I will not allow you to endanger yourself under any circumstances. Do you understand?"

Small white teeth clamped down on a plump lower lip, but she nodded. Satisfied, he straightened, letting his tail curve briefly around her waist as he did.

"Now, shall we work together or shall I take you straight back to the main house?"

He told himself that he did not find her frustrated glare entirely too adorable.

"Fine," she finally snapped. "I'll start in the bedroom."

"I will finish in here and then assist you."

"I don't suppose it would do any good to say I don't need your assistance?"

"No."

"You should have been named Bossy instead of Borgaz," she muttered as she turned to march out of the kitchen.

Bossy? A smile curved his lips as he translated the word.

"I have no objection to being in charge of you."

Before she could react, he turned back to the sink.

CHAPTER 5

What did I do to deserve this, Mary fumed as she cleaned out the front room she had decided to use as a bedroom. Like the rest of the house, it still contained most of their original furniture, shrouded under dusty sheets. All they'd taken with them when they left was one wagonload of possessions, but Matthew hadn't even bothered to sell what remained.

When they had lived here, the front room had been a rarely used formal parlor, but it was spacious enough to make an adequate bedroom. Even without the broken window, her old bedroom was too much of a reminder of the girl she had once been, and she couldn't imagine using her parents' room. The parlor would even have a nice view over the surrounding hills once she trimmed away the overgrown vines.

Assuming Borgaz would trust her with pruning shears. *Impossible male.*

Although it was nice of him to fix that leak. *Maybe I should ask him to look at the hot water generator while he's here...* No. She refused to make the mistake of being dependent on anyone else again.

After her parents died, their neighbor William had stepped in to help deal with the formalities. She'd been so dazed by grief and shock that she'd simply let him take care of everything. It wasn't until the lights stopped working two months later that she realized the credits her parents had left for her were gone.

When she gathered the nerve to confront him, he assured her that they had only been used for expenses she'd approved—expenses she didn't remember. Which only proved that she needed someone to look after her, he told her, and he intended to be that person. He'd been so smoothly convincing that she'd almost agreed, but some inner voice had warned her not to listen.

The next morning she'd slipped quietly out of the house to visit the bank and found that he'd transferred everything out of her account. But all of it had been under her signature and the bank manager, while sympathetic, had been unable to reverse the transactions.

From that point on she'd been determined to rely only on herself. She had nothing left to take—nothing except this land she wanted so desperately—but she wasn't going to take any chances. The sooner Borgaz left, the better.

She'd just finished uncovering the furniture and sweeping the floor when he appeared in the doorway, big, imposing, and scowling.

"You are preparing a room for entertaining?" he asked, taking in the formal sofa and chairs she had uncovered. "Do you expect visitors?"

His tail lashed as he spoke and she shot it a fascinated glance before huffing at him.

"Of course not. I'm going to use this room for sleeping."

"There is no bed."

"I did notice that. I'll just curl up on the sofa for now."

His frown deepened as he studied the velvet-covered couch. With the rich fabric and elaborate carving, the piece had been her mother's pride and joy but it had been designed for looks rather than comfort.

"It is too small, even for you alone. There is a perfectly adequate room for sleeping behind this one. Why not use that?"

"Because it was my parents' room."

She expected him to argue. Instead, he gave her a thoughtful look, then nodded abruptly and disappeared again. He'd actually let her get the last word? Triumphant, she set to work cleaning the windows until the sunlight that filtered through the vines sparkled on the clean glass. She'd just finished when he returned with a big mattress.

"I aired it out and filled it with fresh bedding," he said before she could object. "There should be nothing to disturb you."

The mattress would be far more comfortable than the sofa, and she gave a begrudging nod. Not that he'd waited for her approval—he'd already moved the sofa to one side to make room for the mattress.

"The blankets are airing as well, but vermin used the pillows for nesting. We will bring new ones when we return tonight."

"*We* are not returning. I am returning and I don't need your pillows. If I want some I'll order them from Mr. Armstrong."

Or make her own, given her limited funds, but it wasn't his concern.

Once again he looked at her silently, then disappeared, but this time she didn't feel nearly so triumphant. She had the sinking suspicion that he'd already formed his own plans and had simply decided not to argue.

Finished with the parlor, she moved on to the bathroom, only to find that it had been scrubbed within an inch of its life—and the hot water was working. *Dammit.* Even though she hadn't asked him to fix it, she couldn't deny that it was a relief to know she would have hot water. Sighing, she went to find him.

He was hammering the loose boards on the porch back into place. He'd discarded his shirt, and his muscled back gleamed in the setting sun as he drove a nail home with one powerful blow. *Oh my.* She'd been too scared and then too irritated to pay much attention before, but she couldn't help giving an appreciative glance at all that masculine power.

His tail flicked at her, but he didn't look up.

"These boards should be replaced, but this will render them safe for now. My preliminary inspection did not discover any other structural weaknesses. The plumbing is functional and I have blocked the vermin holes temporarily. If you insist on returning, I suppose it would be safe enough."

"How nice of you to approve," she said dryly, and he sat back on his heels, pinning her with that amber gaze.

"I do not approve. This dwelling will not provide a comfortable environment for a delicate female."

She rolled her eyes.

"The last thing I am is delicate. And compared to the delights of Ma Cantor's Cosmic Boarding House, my home is more than comfortable."

"You were living there?" An unmistakable look of horror crossed his face before it was replaced by the now familiar scowl. "Foolish female."

She didn't entirely disagree, but she hadn't exactly had a choice. She turned to go back into the house, but he reached out and grabbed her hand. His fingers around hers were big and warm and oddly comforting, and she suppressed a not unpleasant shiver.

"Are you ready to visit the main house?"

"I suppose so."

"You do not wish to make some alteration to your appearance?"

"What the hell is wrong with my appearance?"

Annoyed, she tried to pull her hand away but she might as well have tried to escape an iron manacle.

"If I were criticizing you, you would know it, fojii." His expression was solemn, but she was sure she caught a trace of amusement in his voice. "I was merely suggesting that you would probably prefer to refresh your garments after such strenuous cleaning activities."

His gaze traveled down over her shirt and lingered. She couldn't be entirely sure if he was looking at her breasts, or the streaks of dust that discolored the fabric. Her uncertainty didn't prevent her nipples from stiffening under that intense scrutiny but she did her best to ignore them. She tugged on her hand again, and this time he let her go.

"Fine. I'll go and change. I assume you're going to put your clothes back on?"

That was definitely amusement, although it was quickly masked.

"Unfortunately," he agreed, and she headed back into the house with her cheeks burning.

A few minutes later she returned wearing a clean pair of jeans and a pretty pale blue blouse with a wide neckline that brought out the blue in her eyes. Although dresses still seemed to be more acceptable in Wainwright, she only had one other dress and she didn't think Rosie would care. She chose not to think about why she'd opted for her prettiest blouse.

Borgaz was waiting at the bottom of the porch steps, his shirt back on, but it fit snugly enough that it did little to disguise his muscular frame. His tail flicked behind him and his eyes gleamed amber as they swept over her, but his voice was gruff.

"Better. Come, let us leave before darkness falls."

He put a hand on her back to steer her towards the barn. She ignored the warmth radiating from his touch, and the little tingle that went all the way down her spine.

"Where are we—oh!" A big black stallion was waiting patiently beneath the crooked roof. "What a magnificent horse. What's his name?"

She held out her hand to the horse, letting him snuffle it and wishing she had a carrot.

"I don't know. He came with the ranch."

"Matthew may have been a bastard, but he had good taste in horses."

She stroked the soft nose, murmuring to the horse, then suddenly realized the implication of a single horse and stepped back.

"You'll make better time than I will, but I'll be there as soon as possible."

He was frowning again. "Do not be foolish. You will ride."

"You mean you're going to walk?" she asked doubtfully.

"Of course not. We will both ride. The animal is quite capable of carrying us both."

Before she could state her objections in a way that didn't make her sound like a silly schoolgirl, he picked her up and placed her on the horse's back as easily as she would have lifted a pillow. His big hands spanned her waist, more of that intriguing warmth spreading from his touch, and for a second they seemed to linger. But then he released her and sprang easily into the saddle behind her.

She tried desperately to hold herself a little apart from him, but he only sighed and tugged her back against him as he urged the horse into motion. Deciding a struggle would be undignified—as well as useless—she didn't fight him, but she glared up at him over her shoulder.

"You can't just pick me up and put me where you want me!"

Heat glowed in his amber eyes for a moment before he shrugged, his chest rippling deliciously against her back.

"Why not? It was the most expedient way of dealing with the situation."

The wicked grin she'd seen once before flashed across his face, startlingly attractive on that normally grim countenance. His arms tightened briefly in what could have been a hug. She had a feeling he'd enjoyed placing her where he wanted her, and she swallowed. Hard.

"Relax, little fojii. It is just a ride."

His breath brushed against the sensitive skin on the side of her neck, making her nipples tighten again. Her entire body seemed to flush as he chuckled roughly, but she did her best to ignore it, focusing on the road ahead.

CHAPTER 6

I am undoubtedly a fool, Borgaz decided as the horse moved easily along the rough track leading away from Mary's farm. With each step, the soft curve of her ass rubbed tantalizingly against his aching cock. How long had it been since he'd had any interest in a female? Not since those first painful, confused days after the war had ended when he'd realized that the end of the fighting hadn't meant the end of his nightmares. He'd been desperately seeking any respite from the horrors in his dreams, and he had tried seeking solace with various females.

None had helped, and after the third time he woke to find one cowering across the room from him, frightened by his night terrors, he had stopped trying. If those worldly females, used to rough ports and rough males, couldn't handle the scars the war had left, there was little hope that a delicate little human could do so.

She wiggled again, trying to separate their bodies, but the motion of the horse rocked her back against him in an exquisitely torturous caress. In order to distract himself, he pointed to the field next to them with the broken fence.

"What did you keep here?"

"My parents raised cattle—or at least they did until the cattle started mysteriously getting ill or going missing." Her small frame tensed as she looked over at the empty field. "And of course that's when Matthew stepped up the pressure to take his offer."

"Why did he want your land?"

"Who knows? He didn't do anything with it, so I suspect it was more about making himself appear more important than actually increasing his wealth."

"Your parents did not wish to stay and fight?"

"Maybe they would have if it hadn't been for me. They thought I would have more opportunities in Port Cantor." She shrugged. "Maybe they were right. I missed the farm a lot, but my classes were interesting. But then they died and there was no money to continue my education and… Things didn't go well."

He allowed his arms to tighten briefly, offering comfort, and she relaxed a little.

"My parents died when I was young," he found himself saying. "I went to live with relatives in the city. It also did not go well."

His aunt and uncle had taken him in from obligation rather than desire, and they'd never let him forget it. Was it any wonder he'd turned to a gang of fellow misfits? They'd engaged in little more than petty mischief at first, but that changed over time, their exploits growing steadily more dangerous.

When he'd been caught executing one of their schemes, he'd been sentenced to military service instead of jail and discovered a more satisfying way of life—not only an outlet for his restless energy, but one that combined the camaraderie of his former gang with a more useful purpose. Or at least so he had thought, until he was caught up in an endless, meaningless war...

He was so lost in his memories that it took him a moment to realize she was patting his arm sympathetically.

"I'm sorry. It's hard when everything changes, isn't it?"

He was still staring at those small soft fingers on his arm when he came to his senses.

"I adapted," he said gruffly. "What are your plans now?"

She gave him a quick, startled look over her shoulder at the abrupt change of subject, and he almost apologized, but then she shrugged.

"I'm not sure yet. At this point, my goal is mainly to become as self-sufficient as possible. I had to sell my mother's necklace to provide the funds, but I have enough to make it through this first year." He could hear a trace of regret in her voice at the loss before she continued. "Mr. Armstrong is bringing me a cow and calf, a dozen chickens, and supplies for a large garden. If I can manage it, I'll also plant a field of grain and one of corn. That will allow me to provide for myself and give me time to find out what would be profitable on a long-term basis."

It was a sensible plan, but...

"It is too much work for you."

She had relaxed against him as she talked, but immediately stiffened at his statement.

"No, it's not. I can manage."

It was on the tip of his tongue to offer his assistance, but she was not his responsibility—nor had she given any indication that she would welcome his help. He had also made a commitment to Temel to assist in his project, not to spend his time with an ungrateful little female.

He gave a noncommittal grunt, then asked about the history of the valley. She relaxed again as she talked, her body soft and warm against his, the setting sun catching sparks of gold in her brown hair, and despite the throbbing ache of his cock, he was more content than he had been for a very long time. So content that he frowned as the main house came into view, half-tempted to turn away and continue the ride. But Temel had requested his presence, and Mary wanted to see her friend.

The big white house had a welcoming golden glow, light streaming out onto the porch as Temel opened the front door. His face was as expressionless as always, but Borgaz knew him well enough to see the assessing look he cast Mary and the question in his gaze as he turned to him.

"I'm glad you were able to make it back, along with your companion."

He swung down from the horse, then turned to assist Mary. She was already following, and her body pressed briefly against his as he caught her. He heard her startled breath as his erection rubbed against her stomach, and quickly stepped aside.

"This is Mary," he said gruffly. "She claims that Harkan's mate offered to let her return to her parents' farm."

"It's not a claim—it's a fact," she snapped, the pretty pink on her cheeks fading as she gave him an irritated look. "I have her letter in my pocket if you need to see it."

The last remark was addressed to Temel, but he was already shaking his head.

"That is not necessary. I was already aware of the offer, although Rosie thought perhaps you didn't wish to take advantage of it since it had been some time since she wrote to you."

"You see?" she muttered to him, before turning back to Temel with an apologetic smile. "I'm afraid I've moved quite a lot over the past few years. It took a while for her letter to find me."

Temel bowed courteously, his cultured background surfacing. "I am glad that it did. Your friend and her mate are already inside if you wish to join them."

"Of course. That is…" She looked over at him with an unreadable expression, then nodded abruptly. "I can't wait to see her."

She headed up the porch steps without a backwards glance, her luscious ass swaying provocatively in her tight-fitting pants. He took a half-step after her, then turned to face his commander, relieved that the other male was watching him rather than Mary.

"I have a sudden suspicion that your survey did not proceed very far," Temel said dryly.

"No. The foolish female intends to reside in a house that is clearly not suitable. I made some minor repairs to make sure that it was at least relatively safe, although I still do not think it is appropriate. Perhaps she should stay—" He started to say that she should remain with them, but reconsidered, disliking the thought of sharing her company with three other males, even his fellow warriors. "Perhaps she should stay with Rosie."

"I'm sure she's capable of deciding that for herself."

Despite Temel's mild tone, his gaze was uncomfortably discerning, and Borgaz was glad that his skin did not reveal his emotions the way his female's did.

"I doubt it, but it is none of my concern." He took the horse's reins, fighting the urge to follow Mary instead. "I will stable the horse and then join you."

"No need to hurry. Harkan's mate and Kalpar are discussing the correct preparation of a meat dish in extensive detail."

He returned Temel's smile. Kalpar approached food preparation with the same degree of intensity that he did a tactical plan—no doubt it would be a lengthy discussion.

"Thank you for the warning. I will take my time."

He took the horse to the stables at the rear of the house, doing his best to focus on the task as he fought the urge to hurry back to Mary's side. Once the stallion was fed and watered and stabled, he went to the back of the house and stood on the porch outside the kitchen, gazing out over the quiet grounds. The windows of the main house cast golden pools of light into the darkness, the outbuildings heavy shadows against the last faint glow of the sky as night fell. The only sounds were the soft whisper of the breeze and the faint chirping of some night-dwelling insect. The peaceful atmosphere should have soothed him, but instead restlessness tugged at him.

Laughter sounded from behind him, and he looked through the window to see Mary laughing, her face animated and her hands waving as she talked to Harkan's mate. She looked... happy, happier than she had been all day. She belonged here, just as he belonged with his fellow warriors. Once he made sure her farm was safe, he would move on.

His hand fisted on the railing as he once more considered abandoning his mission. Would it really be so terrible to allow Temel to arrange things on his own? There was no doubt that he would do a thorough job, but perhaps—

"She seems like a delightful female."

Temel had silently come up beside him, nodding as he too surveyed the kitchen's occupants.

"Delightful" was not how he would have described her. Intriguing, stubborn, exasperating—

"Have you told her about your difficulties?" his friend added quietly.

"No." He scowled. "And I don't have any. My injuries have all healed."

Temel gave him that same penetrating look, but he didn't argue, even as Borgaz looked away. He had told him of his nightmares once, but it had been long ago and he'd never mentioned it again. He should have known that his commander would remember.

"So you say," Temel said calmly. "But if you intend to court her—"

"I do not." He dragged his gaze away from the sight of Mary's glowing face and forced himself to move away from the window. "I am no fit mate for anyone."

They stared at each other for a long moment, and then Temel shook his head.

"You do not give yourself sufficient credit."

"She deserves better."

Even though the thought of another male courting her brought all his most possessive instincts roaring to life.

"Perhaps she simply deserves to be happy," Temel corrected him, his eyes sympathetic. "And perhaps you do as well. Shall we rejoin the others?" he added without giving Borgaz a chance to respond.

Temel strode into the brightly lit kitchen, and Borgaz followed him.

Both females were still talking animatedly, and Harkan listened with a faintly bemused expression on his rugged face. Borgaz didn't blame him. He'd only exchanged a few sentences with Rosie since they arrived, but she'd proven herself to be just as forceful and opinionated as Mary.

Both females broke off as they entered the room. Temel nodded to them, then went to check on Naffon while Rosie beamed at Borgaz.

"Thank you for helping Mary today."

"I didn't ask him to," Mary muttered, blushing as she looked at him, and Rosie laughed.

"You've been in the city too long. You know that we all help each other out here."

"An admirable sentiment," Kalpar said dryly from his position by the stove. "As long as those offering to help actually know what they're doing."

"There is nothing wrong with cutting the beans the way I do."

"They will be better this way."

Harkan frowned at Kalpar's condescending tone, but Rosie only laughed again.

"Don't worry. I'm perfectly willing to let you cook."

Despite her statement, she levered her pregnant body off her chair to go and inspect what he was doing, Harkan hovering protectively behind her. Her pregnancy had meant little to Borgaz before, but now he found himself picturing Mary ripe with child and an unexpected flash of longing filled him. *No.* He was no fit mate for a female, let alone a fit parent. But when he tore his gaze away and looked down at Mary, perhaps some of that longing remained in his gaze. Something flashed between them, and he took a half-step closer before he came to his senses.

"I need to report," he muttered, and fled.

CHAPTER 7

Impossible male, Mary thought as she stared after Borgaz's departing figure, and yet... There was something about him that appealed to her, something more than that big, muscular body. A sense of connection perhaps.

That's ridiculous. He's an annoying alien warrior and I'm a farmer. As usual, the prospect filled her with a mixture of dread and excitement. She had no illusions about the amount of work involved, but at least she wouldn't be dependent on anyone. And she would never have to leave her home again.

Rosie returned to her side, leaving Harkan at the stove having a low-voiced conversation with Kalpar. The sardonic warrior had intimidated her at first glance, not so much because of his general appearance—he was tall and lean with pale lavender skin—but his glowing silver eyes disconcerted her as he gave her a swift and slightly dismissive appraisal. He became less intimidating when he bent over his pots, and although he had a dry sense of humor, it wasn't malicious.

"I know that dreamy look," Rosie teased.

"No, you don't—unless it's because I'm dreaming of ways to put Borgaz in his place."

"Uh-uh." Her friend was clearly not convinced, her own gaze turning dreamy as she looked over at her mate. "You should give him a chance. They're not like human men."

"You're really happy?" she whispered, even though Rosie's glowing expression left little doubt.

Harkan was also big and intimidating, with minty green skin and dark hair with a slight green tint. He clearly adored Rosie, but he had the same dangerous air that all of the males had. Even Temel, the sternest and most reserved of the males, had it, and the thought of trusting someone like that with her future made her nervous. *Not that I intend to trust anyone with my happiness*, she reminded herself.

"Happier than I ever imagined," Rosie said firmly and although Mary was happy for her friend, she couldn't help a slight pang of envy.

When she had lived in the valley before, Rosie had been the quiet one, too shy to show an interest in any of their neighbors or the men in town. Mary suspected that Rosie's father had been at least partially responsible—he'd always been a mean man, more likely to criticize than praise. Back then, Mary had been the one who was happy to flirt and indulge in hidden kisses behind the barn, or even more than kisses.

Now her friend was the happy, outgoing one, clearly enjoying her relationship with her new alien husband, while Mary felt cold and isolated. Not entirely cold, she amended as Borgaz returned, his eyes immediately going to her and her body flushing with heat despite her best intentions. The feel of his big body behind hers on the ride over was still clearly etched in her mind, not to mention the improbably large erection she had brushed against when she slid down from the horse—an erection for which she was responsible.

Her nipples tingled at the memory, but she shook her head and forced a smile.

"Well, I'm glad you're happy, but I'm not looking for a relationship," she whispered, before looking over at the two males who accompanied Borgaz.

Temel had returned, along with a new alien—another tall male, this one with golden skin and faintly catlike features, the resemblance enhanced by his wild mane of golden hair. Bright blue eyes immediately focused on her face.

"Ah. I heard we had a charming new visitor. I hope this old grouch hasn't ruined your opinion of us."

He elbowed Borgaz as he spoke. Borgaz sighed and cuffed his head, not gently, stepping between the new male and Mary.

"Shut up, Naffon."

Something sparked in Naffon's eyes, and she watched in horrified fascination as his fingers flexed, gleaming claws appearing at his fingertips. He raised one of those clawed hands behind Borgaz's back and she had a sudden terrible feeling that he was planning to return the blow. She started to voice a warning, but then Temel gripped Naffon's shoulder.

"Shall we eat? You would not want to disappoint Kalpar, would you?"

"Wouldn't I? After he made me shovel shit all day?" Despite his embittered words, Naffon relaxed, the wild light dying from his eyes as he grinned at her. "This farming business is not for the weak of stomach."

"No, it's not," she agreed, returning his smile. There was something oddly boyish about him, a strange contrast to the wildness she had just witnessed.

Naffon came to join her at the table but once again Borgaz intercepted him, plunking himself firmly at her side instead. Naffon shot him an amused look, then winked at her and moved on, while Rosie hid a laugh and leaned across the table.

"I was a little scared of them at first too," she whispered, "But they're just big puppies, honestly."

"Puppies with fangs," Mary muttered under her breath, but her friend laughed.

The evening meal proved to be more enjoyable than she anticipated. Everyone crowded around the big wooden table, and the males eagerly dug in to the roasted meat and vegetable stew that Kalpar had prepared.

"This is delicious," she said sincerely.

"It is acceptable." Kalpar frowned at his plate. "I must arrange for additional spices."

"As if I didn't anticipate that," a deep voice interrupted, and she looked up as S'kal, her wagon master, entered the kitchen with a satchel in his hand.

He looked even larger in the confines of the kitchen, but his smile was as friendly as ever.

"Little Mary, I am glad to see you again so soon. I intended to come by and check on you and see if you needed any help."

An odd grumbling noise sounded next to her, and all the males tensed as she turned to look at Borgaz.

"Did you just growl?"

"No." Despite his denial, the barked word was a harsh growl, his eyes fixed on the big newcomer. "Mary does not need your assistance."

S'kal's hands fisted at Borgaz's tone, but he only raised an eyebrow.

"Is that your decision to make?"

Borgaz's body was so tense it was practically vibrating, his chest rumbling, and she poked him with her finger. *Ouch*. It was like poking a boulder.

"Stop that," she muttered before turning back to S'kal. "No, it's not his decision. But although I appreciate the offer, I don't need any help. From anyone."

S'kal dipped his head in acknowledgment before Temel directed him to take a plate and join them. He sat down at the far end of the table, then smiled at her again before digging into his food.

"How do you know him?" Borgaz asked, still growling.

"Not that it's any of your business, but he was the wagon master of the caravan I traveled with. And he was very nice to me so stop being such a grouch."

"He is not a nice male."

"And you are?"

An expression of what looked like sorrow flashed across his face before he shook his head. "No."

She poked him again, more cautiously this time.

"You're not that bad. Just grouchy. And bossy. And—"

Amusement replaced whatever sorrow she had seen as he put a gentle finger across her lips.

"Let us stop there."

She had the oddest urge to flick her tongue across that big finger, to taste him, but she only nodded silently and he removed his finger with a gentle swipe across her lower lip. *Dammit.* Her nipples were tingling again, and when she looked across the table, Rosie was giving her a knowing smile. Ignoring her, she returned to her food with all the dignity she could muster.

After dinner, Temel went over his plans for the farms in the cluster. As they went over the map, she was relieved to see that her farm had been clearly marked, as well as Rosie's. None of the other farms had been claimed because Temel and his males were going to concentrate on the main farm for now. Their reasoning was that it was to acquire knowledge, but she suspected that they were more comfortable together.

"Are you sure you do not wish to join us, S'kal?" Temel asked. "There is plenty of room."

"Nah." The long dark braid swung as he shook his head. "Too restless to stay in one place. And as long as H'zim remains confined to Port Cantor, I will not leave."

Sorrow touched Temel's face.

"Does he see you? He refused to let me visit."

S'kal looked equally grim.

"I haven't given him a choice, although that doesn't mean he actually speaks to me. I talk and he says nothing."

All of the males looked uneasy, and she shot Rosie a puzzled look. Her friend only shook her head, clearly just as confused.

"Very well. But if you change your mind, or encounter any other likely candidates, let me know. In the meantime we will continue with our original plan," Temel concluded, rolling up the map. "Although I would still like that survey completed."

"Yes, Commander." Borgaz was scowling again. "I will not allow myself to be distracted again."

"Distracted?" she whispered furiously. "You were the one who insisted on staying."

"You needed my help. Do you intend to return tonight?" he continued before she could argue.

"Of course I do."

"Then we should leave now."

"I'm quite capable of walking," she assured him. She had no intention of admitting that despite her longing for the quiet of the country, she'd lived in the city long enough to be the tiniest bit nervous about the complete darkness surrounding them.

"I will saddle the horse," he said, ignoring her as usual before disappearing from the kitchen.

She sighed as Rosie came around the table to take his place, frowning at her.

"Don't be so quick to turn down help. We all need it sometimes."

"I don't want to need it. I want to stand on my own."

Rosie's eyes were sympathetic.

"I know, but accepting help when it's offered doesn't mean you can't do it on your own. I managed by myself, but having Harkan by my side changed everything for the better."

"But he's your husband. I'm not looking for a husband."

"Of course not," her friend said solemnly, even though her eyes twinkled. "But you were the one who first told me about all the... fun things that can happen between a woman and a man. And alien males seem to be very blessed in that department."

"There is only one male who should concern you, my mate."

Harkan gave Rosie a mock frown as he came to join them, and she smiled up at him.

"I was just sharing how wonderful you are. Are you ready to go home?"

"Yes. I wish to fulfill your faith in me. As soon as possible."

Rosie laughed and blushed as he lifted her easily into his arms, despite her advanced pregnancy.

"I can walk."

"But I can walk more quickly."

Mary barely had time to say goodbye before Harkan whisked Rosie away, passing Borgaz as he returned.

"The animal is ready."

Since she really didn't want to walk home in the dark, she gave in to the inevitable, turning to thank Kalpar for the meal and saying goodbye to the others.

"It was a pleasure to see you again, little Mary." S'kal bowed his head politely. "If you need anything from Port Cantor, you have only to let me know."

Borgaz growled again and swept her out the door before she could thank S'kal.

"What is with you?" she demanded. "You're like a dog with a bone."

His annoyed expression vanished as he considered her words, clearly translating them in his head.

"You think I wish to feast on you?"

Her mind immediately conjured up an image of that horned head lodged between her legs, and heat pooled in her stomach. Would that really be so bad? It had been a long time since she'd had any interest in men, but her body was undoubtedly responding to Borgaz.

The amber glow in his eyes deepened as he stepped closer and she waited breathlessly. His hands circled her waist, big and strong as they flexed against the soft flesh, so close his delicious spicy scent filled her head. He lowered his head, but instead of touching his lips to her mouth, he brushed them softly against the frantic pulse beating in her neck. An aching rush of sensation washed through her, and she let out a small sigh, trembling against him.

He rumbled with pleasure and repeated the caress, a whisper across her throat, and she wrapped her arms around his neck, leaning into him. Big and strong and comforting. And then he opened his mouth and a soft brush of fangs raked across her sensitive skin. She shivered and he let out a satisfied sound before pulling away abruptly.

"We should go."

Without waiting for an answer, he picked her up and sat her on the horse, then settled himself behind her. This time she made no attempt to try and keep their bodies separate. She let herself lean back against him, inhaling that warm, spicy scent. She could almost imagine the rumble in his chest was a purr as his hand curved around her hip to hold her more tightly.

It was going to be a long, pleasurable ride home.

CHAPTER 8

Borgaz was grateful for the darkness as they rode silently through the night—he suspected his uncertainty would be clearly visible on his face. He had no business putting his mouth on the female in his arms, let alone teasing the tempting pulse of her neck with his fangs. The place where he would put a mating bite, if he were ever to be mated. *Which I am not*, he reminded himself. *I am not a fit mate.*

No matter how sweet and tempting she had been beneath his mouth.

She was no longer wiggling around as she had been on the ride over, trying to separate their bodies, but having her lush ass settled firmly against his erection was just as enticing. He forced his mind away from his cock and onto practical matters.

"Are you tired?" he asked, raising his voice slightly to be heard above the soft clopping of the horse's hooves.

"No." Her denial was immediately followed by a yawn, and she laughed. "Well, maybe a little. And I'll probably be up before sunrise anyway. I'll have to get used to early mornings again."

"I remember. And life in the military was no different. It is only civilians who sleep late and waste the day."

"I don't know. Sometimes it's nice just to be lazy and stay in bed."

Was she trying to be provocative? Did she realize what the thought of a long morning in bed with her did to him? Although he suspected a morning would not be enough. It would take much longer to explore that sweet body, to sate himself on her taste and scent and delicious softness...

He was so lost in the thought that it took him a moment to realize she had asked him a question.

"What did you ask me?"

"I want to know what was going on between you and S'kal. You never answered me the first time."

The taste of her flesh had driven the question from his mind, but the reminder made him frown.

"It is... complicated. He is a member of our squad, so I would have no hesitation in trusting my life to him and have done so in the past."

"But..."

"S'kal has a brother who can be... dangerous, but S'kal's loyalty is to him above all else. It has been a source of conflict between us in the past."

"That doesn't explain why you acted so oddly tonight. Why don't you trust him?"

Trust. It had come hard for him since his parents' death, and while he had learned to trust his squad, that life was no more. And of his fellow warriors, S'kal was the only one likely to be a real rival for Mary's affections. Temel was too focused on his project, Naffon too impetuous, and Kalpar had never shown any interest in a female. But S'kal liked females and females liked him. His familiar greeting to Mary had only reinforced that belief—and he did not like it.

"Trust must be earned," he said briefly as her house appeared and he reluctantly reined in the horse. "You should get some rest."

He dismounted, then reached up and lifted her to the ground but didn't immediately release her. She looked up at him, her eyes grey in the moonlight. Her scent rose to his nose, sweet and almost unbearably tempting.

"I suppose I should thank you for your help today."

The words sounded reluctant, but her voice was soft and slightly breathless.

"I do not want your thanks," he said gruffly.

"What do you want, Borgaz?"

What did he want? For years, the war and his duties to his fellow warriors had given him purpose. With the end of the fighting, that purpose had been taken from him. He'd yet to discover anything to replace it, except perhaps something he could not have.

"It is time for you to enter your dwelling."

The sudden snap to his voice made her jerk back, and he swore softly under his breath as he released her. She was not a soldier and he had no right to speak to her so brusquely. He struggled for the right words to apologize as he followed her up to the repaired porch. The wind rustled in the trees, and something screeched in the distance. She shivered, looking out into the night.

"I had forgotten what it was like at night here."

"If you are afraid, you could return to the main house."

As soon as he said it, he knew it was a mistake. Her back straightened as she gave him an outraged look.

"I'm not afraid."

"Of course not, fojii."

"What does that mean anyway?" she asked crossly.

"It is a small animal from my homeworld. Its fur bristles when it is angry."

Unable to resist, he stroked his hand across the soft silk of her hair and ran her braid through his fingers. He tugged, very lightly, so that she lifted her face to him as her sweet scent deepened. Was she aroused? He tightened his grip a little more and her lips parted, gleaming softly in the moonlight.

"That doesn't sound very flattering," she whispered.

"On the contrary. It is small but very appealing." He wrapped the thick braid around his hand, holding her in place as he bent towards her. "Appealing enough to attract dangerous predators."

His voice was more of a growl now, and he heard the uncertainty in her response.

"Borgaz..."

Her breath feathered across his mouth as he cupped her cheek with his free hand, her skin silky smooth against his callused fingers, and he could no longer resist. He put his mouth against hers, those soft lips pliant beneath his.

He had only intended it to be a light kiss—just a quick taste—but then her lips parted on a surprised gasp and his tongue surged forward to seek hers. His cock throbbed and his horns ached, his body responding to her sweetness. She made a soft sound as his tongue stroked hers, and he realized she was trembling.

Fear or desire? he wondered, and reluctantly abandoned her lips to stare down at her. She looked dazed, her cheeks flushed pink, and he expected to see fear in her eyes, but to his shock and delight he saw only desire.

"Please." It was the merest whisper, but it was enough. He captured her lips again, savoring the taste of her as his arms tightened, and he gave in to the urge to crush her against his body.

She fit perfectly against him, and his tail wrapped around her to bring her closer. *Mine.*

A loud screech came from a nearby tree, the sound startling him, and he whirled around to face the threat, automatically thrusting her behind him. A night creature, he realized a second too late, but his reaction only enforced his fears. He was still a warrior, a damaged one, not a mate.

He turned to find her staring at him, her eyes wide with an expression he couldn't read and her lips pink and swollen. She didn't look afraid, but she should have been.

Reaching into his saddlebag, he pulled out a sack containing the pillows he had promised her and thrust it at her, taking care not to touch her soft, tempting skin as she took it from him.

"You should get inside before I forget all the reasons I should not follow you."

She tilted her head curiously, just as a fojii would have done.

"What reasons?" she asked, then blushed. "Not that I'm asking you to come in."

"I am not a fit mate." The words tasted bitter in his mouth.

There was that unreadable expression again, but then she nodded.

"And I didn't say I was looking for a mate. Good night, Borgaz."

Her fingers brushed lightly against his before she turned and vanished into the house.

"Good night, fojii," he said quietly to the empty porch, then turned to his horse.

He grasped the saddle, then looked back at the house and the surrounding darkness. He couldn't do it. He couldn't leave her here on her own. With a resigned sigh he led the horse into the dilapidated barn and prepared to spend the night.

CHAPTER 9

Mary closed the door behind her and leaned against it, her fingers pressed to her swollen lips. That had been one hell of a kiss. Her whole body felt electrified, alive with excitement, her nipples taut and aching and a low steady pulse throbbing between her legs. He might be grouchy and bossy and annoying, but none of that had mattered when he was holding her against that big, powerful body.

Kissing her, his mouth hot and delicious and commanding.

I wouldn't have stopped him, she realized, and swore. The last thing she needed was to get involved with another man. At least it was just a kiss. She probably wouldn't even see him again unless she went to visit Rosie. Ignoring a pang of disappointment at the thought, she walked into her new bedroom.

A shadow passed in front of the curtains and her heart skipped a beat. She tiptoed quietly to the window, peering out from behind the curtain in time to see Borgaz and his horse disappearing into her dilapidated barn. He wasn't leaving?

She waited, her heart pounding, but he didn't reemerge, and she finally realized he was spending the night in the barn. *Maybe I should invite him in.* Or maybe that would be like inviting the fox into the henhouse to meet an all too willing hen.

Instead, she settled down on her new mattress, smelling deliciously of clean straw and the faintest trace of Borgaz. Another screech sounded from outside and she remembered the way he had whirled around, transforming from lover to warrior. Perhaps it should have frightened her; instead, it made her feel safe. Hugging the pillow tighter she went peacefully to sleep.

As she suspected, she woke as soon as the sky began to lighten. The morning light didn't do the room any favors. She could see a faint stain on the ceiling where the roof must have leaked and a sliver of light next to the window where the frame had warped. She sighed and made a mental note to add both tasks to her ever-growing list.

Rising, she stretched then pushed the curtain aside to look at the barn. She couldn't tell if Borgaz was still there or not. Should she check on him?

After a quick trip to the bathroom to use the thankfully warm water, she dressed and went outside. The spring air still held a hint of winter chill, and she shivered as she crossed to the barn.

The doors creaked when she pulled on them, and she peered cautiously into the interior. Empty. Telling herself she wasn't disappointed, she returned to the house to begin making a list of everything she needed to do and everything she still needed to purchase. Both lists were depressingly long, but she refused to be discouraged. It would be worth it in the end to have her own home that no one could take away from her.

After she finished, she went to inspect the barn. Despite her first impression, other than the warped doors it was in relatively good shape, so she cleaned out two stalls for the cow and calf. Just as with the contents of the house, Matthew hadn't even bothered to take any of the equipment so at least she wouldn't need to replace it. She made a quick inventory and returned to the house to have a fast meal before Mr. Anderson arrived.

She was scrambling the eggs she had brought from Wainwright when she heard a horse nicker and the distinctive creak of the barn doors. Her heartbeat sped up but she did her best to ignore it as she scooped the scrambled eggs out of the pan and into a bowl. A heavy tread on the back porch, and then Borgaz appeared, his big body filling the kitchen doorway. Her heart certainly didn't skip a beat at that scowling face.

"You're back," she said as calmly as possible.

He grunted and came over to look down at her bowl.

"That is all you are eating?"

"It's more than enough for me. I have a few more eggs if you would like some. And some bread. It's not much, but..."

"I will not take what little food you have. I trust you are expecting other supplies?"

"Of course. I told you Mr. Anderson is bringing—" She broke off and gave him a suspicious look. "Is that why you're here?"

He didn't even have the grace to look embarrassed.

"Yes. You are allowing a strange male to visit you."

She crossed her arms and glared at him.

"First of all, he's not a strange male. I've known him most of my life. Second, it's none of your business who comes to see me. Or why they come," she added defiantly. "I might have a lot of visitors once word gets out that I've returned."

His eyes narrowed and he took a step closer, trapping her against the counter.

"What kind of visitors, fojii? Do you intend to start courting?"

She ran her tongue nervously across her lips, and that gleaming amber gaze followed the movement.

"Maybe. It isn't any of your business."

"Yes, it is," he growled, stepping even closer so that his big, hard body pressed against hers.

Her nipples turned to stiff peaks, rubbing against that broad chest, and the glow in his eyes increased.

"Why?" she asked breathlessly. "Why is it your business?"

He opened his mouth, then closed it again, a frustrated expression on his face. Telling herself she wasn't disappointed, she pushed at his chest—to absolutely no effect.

"Stop crowding me."

He growled again, then bent his head and kissed her.

Just a hard, fierce pressure against her mouth at first, but it made her entire body flare with heat. Her hands, which had been pushing at his chest, curled around his neck instead as his mouth opened over hers.

His hands circled her waist, lifting her up onto the counter, and she instinctively wrapped her legs around his hips. She gasped as the heated ache between her legs pressed deliciously against his rigid abs. He wrapped her braid around his hand again as his other hand stroked her neck, then slid down to cup her breast. His touch was delicate, feather light, a shocking contrast to the heated demand of his mouth, and she wriggled restlessly, trying to get closer.

He gave a low, satisfied chuckle against her mouth, holding her in place easily as he feathered a thumb across an aching nipple.

"Impatient little fojii."

His mouth moved from her lips to her neck, teasing the throbbing pulse as he had the night before. The faint scrape of his fangs on the sensitive flesh sent little shivers of excitement coursing through her body, and she tilted her head to allow him better access as she tried to pull him closer. His thumb and finger closed around her nipple, the firm grasp adding to her arousal.

Her hands curved up over his head, tugging on his horns, and he growled again, his mouth sucking harder at her neck as she rocked against him. Her whole body quivered, her muscles tensing, and...

He suddenly snarled, a harsh, vicious sound, and stepped back, leaving her staring at him in shock, her breath still coming in rapid pants. His face was a harsh mask as he returned her gaze.

"I will not do this."

Shock turned into embarrassment and then anger.

"I didn't ask you to kiss me, dammit."

"You did not stop—" He broke off and rubbed a hand over his face. "No, it is not your fault. I am the one who lacks discipline."

Discipline?

Gathering her wounded pride around her like a cloak, she hopped down from the counter.

"It was just a kiss," she said as lightly as possible. "No need to overreact."

"Overreact?"

The familiar frown began to descend, but before he could say anything she caught the steady clop of a horse and wagon. Saved by the delivery cart.

"That sounds like Mr. Anderson. I don't suppose you're just going to let me deal with him on my own?"

She couldn't imagine Mr. Anderson not mentioning the presence of a huge, glowering red alien on her farm, and she winced at the thought of the resulting gossip.

Borgaz's frown deepened, but to her surprise, he nodded.

"I will keep watch."

He left through the kitchen door just as Mr. Anderson knocked on the front door.

"Good morning," she called out as she hurried to open the door, but instead of the shopkeeper, a gangly red-headed man stood there, giving her a bashful smile.

"Hiya, Mary. I don't suppose you remember me?"

She took a second look, then smiled as she recognized him. Ferdie had been her first boyfriend, a very long time ago it seemed now. He was taller, and very slightly broader, but the hair and the smile were unmistakable.

"Ferdie? Is that really you?"

"Yes, ma'am." His grin widened. "I work for Mr. Anderson now."

"So you decided not to leave Wainwright after all?"

Ferdie had been full of big plans when she'd known him, most of them improbable, but they'd both liked to speculate on life outside of the town.

"Nah. I'm married now. And since Nelly got married and moved to the ranch with Commander Artek, Mr. Anderson is going to make me a partner in a few more years."

His casual mention of the alien Nelly had married made her wonder if he would have been as horrified as she had assumed by Borgaz's present. Still, she was just as glad he was out of sight as she smiled at Ferdie.

"Congratulations—on both counts. Do I know your wife?"

"Her name is Agnes. She used to be married to Sam Perdy, but he up and disappeared one spring. I adopted her children, and we have another one on the way."

She had a vague recollection of Agnes, a plain woman with a sweet smile who was several years older than the two of them, but Ferdie looked proud and happy.

"I'm very happy for you both. Once I get this place licked into shape, you'll have to bring her for a visit."

He looked around at the peeling paint and the crooked porch post. He didn't say anything but his doubts were easy to read, and she laughed.

"I know. It may be a long while before I'm ready to receive visitors, but I'd love to talk to you again."

A low grumble sounded from the side of the house, and Ferdie frowned.

"Did you hear that?"

She assumed an innocent expression, hoping Borgaz would keep his word.

"I'm sure it wasn't anything important. Shall we unload the supplies?"

"You just tell me where you want them," he said firmly as he led her over to the wagon.

Her new cow and calf were tied behind it, and she took them into the barn as he began unloading the rest. Sacks of feed and grain to be stored in the barn, a variety of seeds and young plants for her garden, and several boxes of food and supplies. He carried the crate of chickens to their coop, then shook his head.

"You've got holes in the fencing. Better fix that before releasing them. Do you want me to take care of it?"

Behind him, she could see Borgaz standing at the edge of the house, glowering, and she shook her head quickly as she tried to surreptitiously wave him back.

"That's all right, thanks. I can handle it."

"Well, if you're sure, I'd best be getting back."

She accompanied him back to the wagon, and he smiled down at her.

"It's good to see you again, Mary. I'm sorry the city didn't work out for you."

If he only knew... Her smile felt a little more forced this time as she thanked him. She repeated the future invitation, then waved as he drove away down the road.

She turned to go back to the barn and almost ran into Borgaz standing behind her with his arms folded and a frown on his face.

"The human male likes you."

"Only because we grew up together." She wasn't about to share the fact that he'd also been the first boy to kiss her. Actually, she had kissed him, but either way, Borgaz didn't need to know. "And besides, he's married now."

The frown remained.

"I do not trust this marriage of yours. Humans discard those vows too easily."

"And I suppose your people don't?"

"Oh, no." He leaned closer. "When an Erythran claims a mate, the bond is for life."

His eyes dropped to her mouth and her heart started pounding, but then he abruptly turned away.

"I will repair the animal shelter."

Without giving her a chance to respond, he stomped over to the coop and began examining the torn wire mesh. She stared after him and shook her head. *Impossible male.* She briefly considered telling him that she didn't need the help, then decided not to waste her breath and went to eat her now cold eggs and begin putting away the kitchen supplies.

He had clearly decided not to pursue whatever was happening between them and that was just fine with her. She didn't need any more hot, confusing kisses. And she definitely didn't want to be his mate. No matter how intriguing the thought.

CHAPTER 10

*B*orgaz swore under his breath as he finished examining the damage to the chicken enclosure and went to find the tools to repair it. He was showing all the signs of an Erythran in the grip of mating fever, no matter how much he tried to deny it.

I should not have returned.

He had slept little the previous night, his senses as alert as they had been when performing sentry duty during the war. But near dawn he had slipped into a deeper sleep, only to find the horrors of the past waiting for him. He had awoken in a cold sweat, a hoarse cry on his lips and his hand reaching for the blaster he no longer carried. At least he was still in the barn—sometimes his nightmares sent him wandering unknowingly through the night.

His awakening had been a harsh reminder of his deficiencies, and as soon as the first light crept across the horizon, he had forced himself to leave. A brief glance at the dilapidated but peaceful farmhouse had been all he permitted himself before setting off to work on Temel's survey.

However, as the sun approached its zenith the thought of her receiving a human male, alone and unprotected, haunted him and he'd finally decided to return. *Merely to keep watch*, he'd assured himself. But his good intentions hadn't stopped him from entering her house. Nor had they stopped him from kissing her.

His cock throbbed at the memory of her sweetness, of her mouth yielding to his kiss, of her breast soft and full in his hand, of her body moving against his as she stroked his horns... He'd been on the verge of stripping away her clothing and burying himself inside her when he came to his senses. He could not —*would not*—claim her.

Despite that knowledge, he hated watching her talking to the human male, watching her smiling so easily. Only the fact that he'd told her he would keep watch rather than join her kept him away. That and the fact that the male did not touch her. If he had...

He swore as a growl rumbled through his chest. He had to regain control over this impossible need to claim her, to protect her. It didn't help that she was living in such deplorable conditions. Perhaps if he could assure himself that she was safe and her house and farm were in good working order, he would be able to put some distance between them.

With that goal in mind he set to work. Once the chicken shelter was repaired, he moved on to the barn, making sure the doors were working smoothly and easily, before refastening some loose boards. He was hammering the last in place when she came to find him.

He had removed his shirt due to the warmth of the day and heat of his efforts, and he didn't miss the way her eyes trailed appreciatively across his chest. Not that the approving look stopped her from crossing her arms and frowning at him.

"What are you doing?"

"Repairing the loose boards."

"I can see that. I mean why are you doing it? I told you I don't need any help."

He couldn't help smiling at her enraged expression.

"I know, fojii. But this way your supplies will remain safe and dry."

He straightened, allowing himself to stretch lazily. Her tongue touched her pretty lips as she watched him, and his shaft began to stiffen. *No. I am here only to work.*

"I have repaired the shelter for the chickens," he said abruptly, turning away from the tempting sight. "However, I did not release them since I am not aware of what is required for their care."

He heard her exasperated huff before she sighed and thanked him.

"All I need to do now is check the nesting boxes and put down a layer of straw."

"I will get the bale of straw."

He strode away before she could object, his tail lashing behind him.

"I planned to continue work on the porch," he told her once the chickens were settled. He'd made careful note of the process in case he needed to attend to them in future—not that he planned to be around for much longer. "Unless there is something else you wish me to do?"

"I don't wish you to do anything," she muttered.

He waited silently until she sighed.

"I'm going to start plowing the nearest field. The ground is workable, and I want to get the grain planted as soon as possible. Then I'll work on the garden. The house is good enough for now."

He didn't consider it suitable, but he didn't argue.

"What equipment do you have? I do not recall seeing a plow in the tool shed."

"It's in the other barn."

He followed her to the smaller building, then stared in appalled horror at the small tilling machine she showed him.

"You intend to plow the entire field using this?"

The defiant glare was back. "I most certainly do. I know it's going to take a while—that's why I want to get started."

"This is how your family farmed the land?"

"Well, no. There's a larger plow and my father had a team of oxen to pull it, but the one thing Matthew did take was all the livestock. But I've used this for the garden so I know it will work."

"Show me the plow," he ordered.

"Why? You don't have a team of oxen up your sleeve."

He took a step closer and her lips parted, the tempting pulse on her neck fluttering.

"Why do you always argue with me?" he growled, unable to resist sliding his hand down that thick, silky rope of hair.

"Why do you have to be so bossy?"

Because you are mine. Frustrated that he couldn't answer her, he leaned down and covered that tempting mouth with his instead.

This time he took it slowly, savoring the taste of her and the little breathless sound she made when he tightened his grip on her braid. One of her hands flattened against his bare chest, and he fought the urge to urge it downward to his aching cock. To feel those soft little fingers on his swollen flesh…

He swore under his breath and jerked away. So much for his attempt to remain in control.

"Show me the plow."

"I will not."

Her voice was just as stubborn as his, although her cheeks were flushed and her lips were swollen. She yielded so deliciously to his kiss, but as soon as he raised his head her obstinacy returned. Perhaps he just needed to kiss her longer…

Forcing himself to ignore that delightful prospect, he simply nodded and strode deeper into the small barn. If she would not tell him, he would find it himself. The second section of the barn contained a variety of equipment designed to be pulled by mechanical equipment or beasts of burden. They were not identical to the ones he had seen as a child, but close enough.

"You see?" Mary had followed him, and now she gave a triumphant smile. "They're all useless without a team."

Hmm. He picked up the tongue of the plow and tugged experimentally. Heavy, but not unmanageable. Her eyes widened as she watched him.

"You can't possibly be intending to pull that yourself!"

He was almost tempted to show her that he was quite capable of doing so, but he put aside his pride and shook his head.

"No, but in case you've forgotten, I do have a horse."

"A riding horse."

He shrugged. "We shall see. If not, then I will become your beast of burden."

She muttered something under her breath, but he ignored her and went to get his horse. It required some adaptation of the gear, but his horse stood patiently as he adjusted it and proved willing to pull the plow.

"I should have known," she sighed when he couldn't resist a satisfied smirk.

"Yes, you should have, little fojii. Now I will start on the field."

"Thank you," she said begrudgingly. "Then I'll start on the garden."

He wanted to protest, to tell her to wait and let him do it, but that was an argument he was sure he would lose. He forced himself to nod and head for the field. It was hard but pleasant work, the warmth of the sun on his skin relieved by a slight breeze and the rich scent of freshly turned earth in his nostrils. Birds sang in the trees lining one side of the field, and every time he turned to work his way back towards the house, he could see Mary working in the kitchen garden.

Despite her small size, she worked steadily, moving back and forth across the garden behind the ridiculously small tiller. Her hair started to come loose from its braid, strands catching the light as they floated around her head in the breeze. Her face was flushed but she was smiling, and a curious ache filled his chest. As a child, this was how he had envisioned his future. He had never thought to leave the farm, let alone become involved in a terrible endless war.

The memory disturbed his enjoyment and he forced himself to concentrate on his work. This was not his future; it was only a temporary break from what he had become. He focused on the neat rows of dirt, and when he finally looked back towards the garden, she was gone. Just as well.

The low rays of the setting sun were slanting across the field and the breeze had turned cold when he decided to stop. More than half the field had been plowed, and he didn't want to tax the horse with the unaccustomed labor. He detached the plow and led the horse back to the barn, brushing him down, then providing him with food and water.

"Excellent work today, Arros," he said, surprising himself with the name as he stroked the silken flank. Arros was the name of the zebard he had ridden as a child. A foolish sentiment, but he smiled as he repeated it.

Through the open barn doors he could see a light glowing in the kitchen window and after a brief argument with himself, he went to find Mary. She was standing at the stove, but she flashed a quick look at him over her shoulder as he entered.

Somewhat to his surprise, she didn't immediately order him to leave but merely nodded.

"I made vegetable stew and cornbread. Go and get cleaned up before we eat."

"You cooked for me?"

"I cooked for me, but I made enough for you as well." Her eyes trailed over his body before she grinned. "At least I hope I did."

"I do not want to take your food," he said stiffly.

"And I didn't want you to help me, but here we are." She raised a challenging eyebrow, but when he didn't respond, she pointed towards the hallway. "Clean up. Take advantage of the hot water you fixed. Then eat. That isn't too difficult, is it?"

He shouldn't stay, not in the warm kitchen with the delicious smells, and the even more delicious female. Not even in the cozy, rundown house. But he still found himself walking in the direction she indicated. A simple meal wouldn't hurt anything, would it?

But when he returned to the kitchen and found the table set, big bowls of stew steaming gently, a golden mound of cornbread in the center of the table, and Mary smiling at him, the bone deep longing in his chest was almost as painful as the injuries he had incurred during the war. He hesitated, still debating the urge to run, but she pointed at the chair next to her.

"Now sit. Eat."

"I believe you are the one being bossy now," he muttered as he obeyed, and she laughed.

"Good. It's about time the tables were turned."

He took a large spoonful of stew and almost moaned with pleasure.

"This is delicious."

Her cheeks turned pink as she smiled at him.

"Thank you. I enjoy cooking. I even tried working in a restaurant once in Port Cantor."

Her pleased expression faded.

"What happened?"

"The usual. Another bastard of a boss. He wasn't that bad to me because he liked my cooking, but there were a couple of young Satian girls working there and he treated them like slaves. I finally told him off and he fired me." She shrugged, but he could hear the bitterness in her voice. "I was never very good at keeping my mouth shut and just going along with things."

He couldn't help laughing, despite his anger at the male who had treated her so poorly.

"No, little fojii, I don't imagine you are." She grinned back, her bitterness fading, and his curiosity got the better of him. "What other employment did you seek?"

As they ate she told him about the many jobs she had attempted. Although she kept her voice light and made the stories amusing, he could read between the lines enough to know that she'd had a difficult time. If only he had encountered her then, perhaps he could have aided her. Or perhaps he would have avoided her as she appeared to have avoided other males. Although she let very little drop, he gathered that her attempts at a relationship had been as disappointing as her attempts at employment.

After dinner, they sat at the table drinking tea and to his surprise, he found himself telling her about some of his jobs. There had been fewer and they had lasted longer, but they had been just as unsatisfying.

"Temel was always looking for better opportunities for us, but none of us fit in well in civilian society. Except perhaps S'kal," he admitted reluctantly.

"He seems to enjoy leading the caravans."

"Perhaps. Or perhaps he prefers the constant movement rather than having time to reflect. None of us were unscathed by the war," he added, meeting her eyes across the table.

He saw the understanding on her face before she nodded and rose.

"I'll just clean the dishes—" A wide yawn interrupted her words and she grinned. "And then I'm going to bed."

"I will clean the dishes," he said firmly as he stood. "You need to rest."

Instead of arguing, she tilted her head and considered him thoughtfully.

"Are you planning to spend the night in the barn again?"

She knew about that? He started to deny it and tell her he wouldn't stay, but he already knew he wouldn't be leaving.

"Yes."

"That's stupid, especially after you worked so hard today." She held up a hand when he started to object. "Just stay with me. In the house, I mean," she added quickly, her cheeks turning pink.

"You can stay in my parents' room or upstairs in my old bedroom if you put something over the broken window."

This is not a good idea, he told himself, but he nodded anyway.

"Good, then that's settled." She hesitated again, then rose up on her toes to brush her mouth gently against his. "Thank you for your help today."

He clenched his fists at his side to prevent himself from pulling her closer and demanding more. His tail lashed unhappily as he watched her walk to the door. She looked back long enough to grin at him.

"Not that I need the help, of course."

And then she was gone, leaving him amused, aroused, and entirely too happy to be staying.

CHAPTER 11

A week later, Mary stood to stretch and ease her aching back. She'd spent the morning working on the ancient irrigation system, and she was hot, frustrated, and sore. The day was unusually warm, and the pipes were choked with rust and neglect.

I should have waited for Borgaz.

The insidious thought snaked into her mind, but she immediately rejected it. *No.* She was still determined not to depend on him. The last week had been... confusing.

She hadn't been surprised when she woke the morning after she'd invited him to spend the night in the farmhouse to find him gone. He'd obviously had his doubts about remaining. But a little after noon he'd come riding back and returned to plowing the field. He'd stayed for dinner that night and once again stayed in the farmhouse, and that had become the pattern of their days.

Because of his help she'd made much faster progress than she'd hoped, but although she'd stopped trying to prevent him from helping her, she didn't want to rely on it. He'd never given any indication that he intended to do more than help her get the farm running. And even though he spent each night in the other bedroom, he left no traces of his presence when he departed each morning.

He'd opened up a little more during their long nightly conversations, but only a little. He told her more about his childhood —a childhood very similar to her own—but less about the clearly troubled time after his parents died. He talked about his fellow warriors, but never about the war, shutting down completely the one time she tried to bring it up.

But despite the separate bedrooms and the distance he clearly tried to keep between them, there was a constant and increasingly frustrating thread of sexual tension running between them. She could see the hunger in his eyes when he looked at her, and she was far from oblivious to his powerful body or that rare, wicked smile. And then there were the kisses—three to be exact.

The first had occurred when she had tripped over a hidden root as they inspected the plowed field. He'd caught her, those big arms pulling her tight against his body. Her nipples instantly stiffened, turning to aching points, and he'd noticed, amber eyes gleaming before he groaned and kissed her. The world went up in flames as soon as his tongue delved into her mouth, and when he'd lifted her into his arms, her legs had automatically wrapped around his waist as he settled her over a huge, perfect erection. She'd been rocking desperately against him and he'd been helping her move when he suddenly growled and raised his head.

"Temel is coming," he said, his gaze fixed on something in the distance before looking back down at her. "Perhaps it's just as well."

"Easy for you to say," she snapped as he put her back on her feet, equal parts aroused and embarrassed.

"No, fojii, not easy at all."

He pressed her hand briefly to the very apparent evidence of his own arousal. Her fingers tightened automatically, trying to grasp more of him, and he growled again before turning away to go and greet Temel.

She'd half-expected the commander to be displeased that Borgaz was spending so much time with her, but instead he looked… satisfied. She wasn't sure she liked that either, but she made polite conversation as she served him tea and he told her more about their progress on the main farm.

After he left, she'd hoped that Borgaz would kiss her again, but instead he'd gruffly excused himself and gone off to muck out the cow's stall. *Not that I care if he'd rather deal with cow shit than kiss me*, she thought defiantly as she went about her own chores.

Both of the other kisses had been similar—accidental touches that flared quickly and wildly out of control—and each had been interrupted. Once by more visitors, Rosie and Harkan that time, and as much as she enjoyed seeing her friend she could have wept with frustration.

The second time had been more troubling. He'd actually gone as far as pushing her shirt aside that time, his mouth closing over her nipple with a wonderful wet sucking heat as she clung to his horns. Then a low rumbling had come from overhead, and she was on the ground, Borgaz crouched over her, his eyes on the sky as his fist clenched at his waist, clearly reaching for something that wasn't there.

"What is it?" she whispered, her heart pounding as she pulled her shirt back together.

"Enemy ship. Remain still."

Enemy? She managed to peer over his shoulder to see the stubby winged transport that Artek had arranged to visit twice a year. The cost of air transport was normally prohibitive, but the ranch had established a trading relationship with the port that made the biannual visits worthwhile.

"It's just a transport ship."

He didn't seem to hear her, his face harsh and his eyes fixed on the disappearing ship.

"Borgaz," she said gently, grabbing his wildly thrashing tail and giving it a gentle stroke. "You don't need to worry about that ship."

He turned and snarled at her, his fangs flashing, and she was almost afraid, but she refused to let go of his tail, stroking it again.

"You're safe."

Her words finally penetrated, but instead of relaxing he only looked appalled. He'd muttered an apology and left, not returning until that evening. He refused to discuss the incident and refused to eat dinner with her. He'd even slept in the barn that night, and she'd spent half the night awake and worried.

The next day he acted as if nothing had happened, and for once she'd chosen not to confront him, happy when he joined her in the kitchen as usual that night.

"Definitely a confusing week," she muttered to herself as she sighed and returned to the irrigation system. Confusing and frustrating. She'd been desperate enough to try relieving the pressure herself, but her own hand was a poor substitute for what she really wanted.

That frustration resulted in a particularly forceful tug, and the pipe unexpectedly gave way. She stumbled backwards, then caught her foot on a concealed rock and tumbled to the ground, a sharp pain shooting through her ankle.

Fuck, that hurt. She instinctively reached for her ankle, then winced as she touched it. She tried to stand, but as soon as she put any weight on her foot, a shooting pain ran up through her leg and she collapsed back down. Tears of pain and frustration threatened, but she refused to give in to them, looking around for anything she could use to help bear her weight.

Instead, she saw a huge red figure striding towards her. Thank God.

"Oh, fojii, what have you done to yourself?"

He spoke gruffly, the familiar frown on his face, but his big, warm hands were gentle as he examined the rapidly swelling ankle.

"I... I don't think I can walk."

"Do not even try," he ordered and scooped her up in his arms, carrying her like an infant.

She was aware enough of his strength not to be surprised at the ease with which he carried her back to the house, and she tucked her head against his neck, breathing in his warm, familiar scent. Despite the throb of her ankle, thinking about their kisses had left a lingering arousal and she couldn't resist extending her tongue for a quick lick to see if he tasted as delicious as he smelled.

He growled, his step stuttering for a second.

"Do not distract me."

"Sorry."

Not sorry at all. In fact, she put her mouth back on his neck, sucking gently at the throbbing pulse, the same way he always did to her.

He tugged warningly on her braid, but that only added to the thrill. The ache between her legs was beginning to equal the ache in her ankle, especially when his chest vibrated against her and his tail came up to wrap around her waist. She clutched it as she kissed his neck again, harder this time, and he hissed.

"I will not warn you again, fojii."

She hummed what might have been an assent as she moved higher, seeking the sensitive spot just below his ear and scraping her teeth against it. His pace increased, carrying her rapidly into the house and the small, informal sitting area. He placed her quickly but gently on the overstuffed couch and unwound her arms from around his neck before taking a step back and scowling at her.

She ignored it, smiling at his very obvious erection instead. *Good.* Now both of them were frustrated.

"You chose a poor time for games, little fojii."

Crossing her arms over her chest, she returned his glare.

"I'm playing games? You're the one who keeps kissing me and getting me all excited and then stopping."

His expression changed, becoming so feral that her heart stuttered even as she felt an answering heat surge between her legs. She took a quick, ragged breath, her hands clenching as she watched him stalk towards her. His eyes gleamed a brighter gold than she'd ever seen, his lips peeled back to reveal his fangs.

Her breath came in rapid pants as she waited, but then he brushed against her ankle and she couldn't help crying out. His expression immediately changed to guilt.

"I will tend to your ankle."

Dammit. She bit her lip as he gently removed her shoe and probed her ankle again before giving her a quick, reassuring smile.

"It is sprained rather than broken. I will bind it for you."

He left briefly, returning with a roll of bandage and a jar of pungent-smelling ointment.

"Where did that come from?" she asked suspiciously.

"I always carry a medical kit."

Oh. She bit her lip and refrained from comment as he carefully rubbed the ointment over her ankle. A soothing warmth immediately began to penetrate, increasing when he wrapped the bandage tightly around the swollen flesh.

He gave a satisfied nod, then rose and left the room without another word. He was leaving her? *I shouldn't have teased him,* she thought as she looked at the empty room. Despite all her insistence of being independent, she didn't want to be alone right now. The combination of exhaustion from the morning's work, the pain of her injury, and the frustration of her unsatisfied arousal was too much. A tear slid down her cheek, followed by another, then another.

By the time he returned carrying a tray, she was sobbing.

"Mary, what's wrong? Is the pain worse?"

"You left me," she wailed.

Emotions washed across his face too quickly for her to read, but then it softened. He returned to the couch, picking her up and sitting back down with her in his lap. His tail curved around her waist as he gently stroked her back.

"I did not leave you. I went to make you a cup of tea."

"You didn't tell me."

She knew she sounded ridiculously pathetic, but she didn't care.

"I didn't tell you because I assumed you would argue."

"No, I wouldn't." He gave her a disbelieving look and she couldn't help smiling, wiping impatiently at the tears still dampening her cheeks. "Well, maybe a little."

He laughed and then he kissed her. *Oh, God.* Her pain and frustration melted away as that hot, rough tongue explored her mouth, slowly, thoroughly, setting her on fire with longing. His hand slid down to play with her nipple and she gasped, pulling back from the kiss to glare at him.

"If you leave me hanging this time, I swear I will murder you in your sleep."

"I will take care of you," he promised, then kissed her again before she could think of any more threats.

As he kissed her, he deftly unbuttoned her shirt, then slid his hand up beneath her camisole. His hands too were warm and rough and wonderful. He pushed her gently back against the cushions, then grasped her wrists in one big hand, raising them over her head as his mouth went first to her neck, making her squirm eagerly as his fangs scraped her pulse.

Then he moved lower, tugging her nipple into his mouth, and it was as hot and wet and delicious as she remembered. She could almost have come from that alone, but she wanted more. She tried to arch towards him, to rub her needy clit against that big hard body, but the movement jarred her ankle and she winced. He immediately raised his head.

"Be still and let me care for you," he ordered.

"Bossy."

He grinned at her muttered protest, but then he moved lower, his big hand skating across her bare stomach and making her shiver with excitement. He hesitated when he reached her jeans, but before she could urge him on, he gently unfastened them. Somehow he managed to slide them off, along with her panties, without hurting her ankle, leaving her bare and exposed to that heated amber gaze.

"Beautiful," he growled, and then he was parting her with his tongue, long, hard laps that had her hips trying to rise as she sobbed with relief and need. He grabbed her thighs, holding her firmly in place as he pulled them further apart and the restraint only added to her excitement.

"My delicious little fojii."

His voice rumbled against her sensitive flesh, adding to the sensation of his tongue and mouth, as he adjusted the position of his hands. A thick finger suddenly pressed deep inside her as he began to suck on her clit.

Her breath caught as she froze, her whole body taut with anticipation. Then he sucked harder, his fangs scraping the delicate flesh, and his finger plunged in and out of her as her climax hit. The release shuddered through her, her hands clutching desperately at his horns as she tried to move and couldn't and somehow that only prolonged her climax, the waves of pleasure rolling on and on until she was too limp to move. He finally raised his head, his eyes gleaming gold and that wicked smile on his lips.

"Are you satisfied now?"

She waved a hand, too drained to speak. He pulled his finger free, and she almost moaned at the loss. Another pulse of excitement coursed through her drained body as he sucked the shining digit into his mouth and hummed. She tried to move and accidentally flexed her ankle. He immediately frowned when she winced again.

"I'm fine," she assured him. "My ankle doesn't really even hurt anymore."

He made a disbelieving sound, even as he gently stroked her leg with his tail.

"You should have been more careful, or waited for me to assist you."

A sudden wave of weariness washed over her, and she yawned as her eyes began to close.

"Can't depend on you," she murmured, already half asleep, then forced her eyes open. "Don't leave me now."

"I won't."

It sounded like a vow, and she smiled as she let sleep carry her away.

CHAPTER 12

*B*orgaz made another adjustment to the irrigation system, then nodded with satisfaction as water began to flow through the pipes. Many of them still needed to be replaced, but enough remained intact to water the grain field and the garden. He would have to extend them once the corn was planted.

Dusk was settling in as he rose, but he'd kept his word. He'd remained with Mary as she slept, surprisingly content just to watch over her until she awakened. The fact that she seemed almost surprised to see him bothered him more than it should, and he immediately sought refuge in action.

"Will you be all right on your own? Only for a little while," he added quickly. "But I want to take a look at those pipes before it grows dark."

He almost hoped she'd object, but after a second, she nodded.

"Of course. I'm fine now. You don't even need to come back if there's something else you need to do."

"I will be back," he promised.

After making her a fresh pot of tea and settling her with a book and a blanket, he headed for the field, grateful for a chance to examine his thoughts without her tempting presence to distract him. Even though his cock still ached with frustrated desire, giving her pleasure had been the most satisfying sexual experience of his life. He licked his lips, seeking a last taste of her. Or perhaps not last. Would she permit him to pleasure her again?

His poor cock jerked at the thought, but he would happily trade his satisfaction for hers, especially since he knew he couldn't take things any further. If he entered her, or gods forbid, gave her a mating bite, he would never be able to leave her. And she deserved so much better...

He sighed as he returned to the farmhouse. His attempts to maintain a distance between them had failed, and yet he couldn't regret what had happened. He would just have to try again. *Polite but distant is best for both of us*, he told himself, ignoring the ache in his chest at the thought.

His good intentions vanished the second he stepped into the kitchen and found her hobbling across the floor.

"What the hell do you think you're doing?" he roared, picking her up.

The kitchen table was the nearest flat surface, and he placed her carefully on top of it while he lectured her.

"Do you want to cause permanent damage to your ankle? I told you to stay off of it."

"Oh, pooh. It barely hurts and I was hungry. I'm sure you are too."

"I would have cooked dinner if you had just waited. You are too impatient, fojii."

"You can cook?" she asked, ignoring the reprimand.

"Well, no. But I can grill sandwiches and heat leftovers."

"You never leave leftovers."

Her eyes twinkled, blue in the lamplight, and she looked so pretty that his breath caught in his throat. She had changed clothes, he realized, donning a long white garment with thin straps that left her pretty shoulders bare. The material was so thin that he could see the shadow of her areolae beneath the cloth. As his gaze traveled over her, her nipples tightened, tenting the material.

"You changed clothes."

His voice came out as a hoarse growl, and she gave him a slow, seductive smile, leaning back a little to make her breasts even more prominent.

"I didn't want to try and pull pants up over my ankle, and if I was going to have to stay in bed I decided I might as well be comfortable."

She shrugged, which did spectacular things to her breasts and he couldn't help staring, the blood rushing to his cock so fast his head swam.

"Do you like my nightgown?" she asked, running a finger along the lace edging the low neck.

His eyes tracked the movement of her finger as a soft growl rose in his throat.

"Yes," he snarled, moving forward to grab that teasing finger. *Fuck.* Her hands were so small and her skin so soft. "I like the nightgown. I would like it even more off of you."

She made a small noise of encouragement, but he moved away, turning to lean heavily on the sink as he tried to get himself under control. He couldn't risk touching her, not so soon after what had happened earlier. Not without losing control.

"We should not be doing this."

"Why not?"

The stubborn tone he recognized so well had returned and he turned around to find her frowning at him.

"I do not wish to hurt you, or—"

"My ankle is fine. I promise I'll be careful, and if you don't believe me, you can just keep me from moving. I liked that."

Her voice had turned husky and the aching need was back, pulsing through him so strongly he thought his chest might explode. He moved closer, unable to resist.

"That's not what I meant. I cannot offer you what you need. What you deserve."

Her eyes darkened as she studied him.

"You gave me what I needed earlier."

"And that is all you need?"

He saw the flicker of hesitation before she raised her chin defiantly.

"Yes. I already told you that I don't want to be dependent on anyone. That doesn't mean we can't enjoy ourselves, does it?"

The temptation to agree almost overwhelmed him, but he didn't think it was that simple. For either of them. He would love nothing more than to believe he could remove that pretty gown and lay her back on the table, to feast on her until they were both sated, and be able to walk away before he showed her just how badly he was damaged. And despite her claim, he didn't believe she would be happy with that either.

"I... I think we should have dinner," he said, cowardly avoiding an answer. "Then you should rest."

She frowned, but to his surprise she didn't argue with him, only refusing to let him take her back to the couch while he cooked. Instead, she watched as he placed thick slabs of cheese between the bread she'd baked, then grilled them in butter before handing her one. She moaned appreciatively as she took a bite, then devoured it greedily.

"A feast fit for a king."

"My mother used to make these for me when I was a child."

"What was she like?"

A smile curved his lips as he remembered. "Sweet, gentle, pretty."

"Not argumentative or opinionated?"

Was she teasing him or looking for reassurance?

"No, but my father was also very mild-mannered. As I might have been if they hadn't died and I had remained on the farm."

"You?" Her eyes swept over him with an appreciative warmth that heated his blood before she shook her head. "I'm not sure you were ever meant to be a mild-mannered farmer."

"Such a male would have been a better fit for you," he pointed out, but she was already shaking her head.

"If that's what I wanted, I could have stayed with Ferdie. Or married John Garcia when he asked me."

He growled, suddenly annoyed.

"I do not wish to hear of the other males who wanted you."

"But I didn't want them. Maybe I was waiting for a big, bossy male with horns and a tail and a very wicked tongue."

His cock surged at her words and he bit back a groan. He wanted so much to believe that her words were the truth, but…

"I do not believe this is wise."

"Maybe not. But I want to enjoy our time together, however long it lasts."

She gave him a teasing smile, but it was the vulnerability in her eyes that he couldn't resist. He lifted her onto his lap and kissed her.

Her hands were trapped between them as he plundered her mouth, and she made soft, eager noises as he deepened the kiss, relishing her sweetness. He was so lost in the kiss that it took him several seconds to realize that her hand had found its way under his shirt, her small fingers stroking his abdomen.

He caught her hand, breaking off the kiss as he moved it away.

"Fojii—"

"It's not fair if you get to touch me and I don't get to touch you," she argued, and he closed his eyes, his control slipping.

"I will remove my shirt. Just my shirt."

He released her hand and tugged his shirt over his head. Her soft little hands immediately returned to his chest, leaving trails of fire across his skin as she explored.

"You're so smooth and warm," she murmured, her breath feathering across his nipples and making him shudder.

But then she found the ragged scars across his ribs and he tensed.

"Still beautiful," she said firmly, but to his relief she moved on, drifting down across his abdomen to tease a line along the edge of his pants. His cock was so stiff that the head was only millimeters away from her fingers.

"We could take these off too. After all, you saw me without any clothes at all."

He'd never wanted anything more, but he shook his head. If he removed them he was quite sure he would be buried inside her sweet little body within seconds.

"And I wish to see you without them again."

She gave a disappointed sigh, but willingly raised her hands over her head to let him strip off her nightgown.

"Fuck, you're beautiful."

Pink flared in her cheeks as she gave him a shy smile and he couldn't resist any longer. He swept the dishes off the table and laid her back against it just as he had imagined earlier. Her pale body gleamed against the dark wood, her breasts also flushed pink and topped with perfect little nipples only a few shades darker. The delicate folds beneath the soft brown curls were also pink and glistening with excitement.

"Mine," he growled, the words slipping out before he could prevent them.

"Yes," she agreed, as he bent his head to her breast, and his heart skipped a beat.

For now, he reminded himself. Only for now.

The taste of her skin intoxicated him, and his head spun as he wrapped his tongue around one tempting bud and tugged lightly, then moved to the other. When he lightly pinched her neglected nipple between his fingers, she arched towards him with a low moan and he smiled against her breast, tightening his grip as the scent of her arousal deepened. He teased her until she was writhing beneath him and then he shifted lower.

As soon as he ran his tongue over the hot pink flesh, she cried out, her hands clutching at the sensitive base of his horns. He groaned as he held her in place, feasting hungrily as she trembled beneath him.

"Will you come for me, fojii?"

"God, yes!"

He slid a finger deep inside her hot, silken channel, almost impossibly tight, but she would need to take more and he slowly worked a second finger into her. He curled both fingers upwards and she sobbed and came apart, gripping his fingers in long, milking pulses that made seed leak from his aching cock. His free hand had actually grasped the fastening of his pants before he forced himself to stop and ignore the angry throbbing.

Instead he concentrated on the tight clasp of her sweet cunt around his fingers, on the delicious scent of her arousal, and on the way her eyes shone when she looked up at him. *Mine*, he thought again, but this time he retained enough control not to say it aloud.

He brought her to another trembling peak before reluctantly pulling away and lifting her into his arms. She snuggled against him, her face flushed and relaxed, as he carried her to her bedroom and placed her gently on the mattress. When he started to rise, she reached for him.

"Stay with me."

He knew it was a mistake, but he nodded anyway and slipped into bed next to her. She immediately curled into him with a contented sigh and quickly fell asleep. He did not, staring into the darkness as he tried to memorize every moment of their time together, of the way she looked and tasted and smelled, of the way her eyes snapped with anger or darkened with desire. Memories that would have to sustain him through the long, lonely years ahead.

CHAPTER 13

Mary was not entirely surprised when she woke up alone. No doubt the barriers Borgaz was so determined to erect between them were firmly back in place.

And this is just temporary, she reminded herself, ignoring the ache in her chest at the thought. At least the latest step in their relationship meant that she was feeling a lot less frustrated. She stretched lazily, enjoying the slight ache between her legs and the way her swollen nipples tingled as they rubbed against the sheet.

She did regret that it had stopped with him pleasuring her, but at least she had managed to get him this far. If the size of his erection was anything to go by, he wanted her as much as she wanted him. Surely it wouldn't be too hard to push him that little—or not so little—bit further.

Placing a foot tentatively on the ground, she was delighted to find that her ankle felt much better. It was still tender, but she could walk without too much pain and she hobbled her way to the bathroom. She had just settled into the tub when the door burst open and Borgaz appeared, scowling.

"What are you doing in here? Why didn't you wait until I could help you?"

"Because I'm perfectly capable of walking," she said calmly, and mostly truthfully. "But you're welcome to help me bathe if that makes you feel better."

His eyes dropped to her wet breasts and her already erect nipples and he swallowed hard. His erection tented his pants, but he shook his head.

"Not unless you need my help."

"Don't you want to make sure I'm really clean?"

She cupped her breast, offering it to him, but although the amber light glowed in his eyes, he shook his head, muttered something unintelligible, and backed out of the bathroom as quickly as he entered it. She sighed, but she really hadn't expected him to succumb that quickly. She was still convinced he wanted her as much as she wanted him. It was simply a matter of time.

THREE DAYS LATER SHE WAS CONSIDERABLY LESS SANGUINE about the prospect. Their routine hadn't changed—except for the admittedly delightful fact that he went to bed with her each night, discovering ever more pleasurable ways of satisfying her. But he never remained after she fell asleep, and he still hadn't let her touch him despite his obvious desire.

She was scowling at his distant figure as he planted grain when she was distracted by the sound of an approaching horse and wagon. Since she hadn't ordered anything else she tensed, but knowing Borgaz was nearby gave her the confidence to wait calmly until the wagon was close enough to recognize the occupants. Rosie and Harkan.

She smiled and went to greet them as Harkan carefully lifted Rosie down from the wagon.

"Rosalie wished to see you, but she tires easily. Don't let her exert herself," he ordered, and Rosie rolled her eyes.

"I'm just fine. Now go talk to Borgaz while I talk to Mary."

"I would rather stay with you."

"And I would rather talk to Mary alone. Now shoo."

Mary couldn't help smiling as he gave a disgruntled nod and walked towards the field, remembering shooing Borgaz along the same way, but then she gave her friend a curious look.

"Is something wrong?" she asked.

"That's what I came to ask you. I know Borgaz is staying here, even though you said you weren't interested, so I thought I'd check up on you." Rosie studied her face as she blushed. "I take it you want him here?"

"Of course I do. He wouldn't stay if I didn't. Well, he might," she added as she led the way back into the house. "If he thought I needed help. But he's not forcing himself on me or anything like that."

Unfortunately.

"Do you want him to?" Rosie's eyes twinkled, clearly picking up on her disgruntled tone.

"It's complicated."

"It always is." Her friend sighed with relief as she collapsed into a kitchen chair. "I swear this baby is going to weigh at least fifteen pounds. He gets heavier every day."

Her eyes widened. "Really?"

"No, not really. Drakkar—he's one of the original aliens at the ranch and my doctor—assures me that he is of perfectly normal human size even if his daddy is a giant. He said it's some kind of adaptation to mixing our species."

"You didn't have any problems getting pregnant?"

Rosie laughed. "Nope. I said I wanted a baby, and Harkan immediately obliged. I think I was pregnant the next day."

She couldn't help a wistful sigh. At least someone was getting some.

"Now what was that about?" her friend demanded. "You were the one who had to convince me that sex was fun. Although it really wasn't until I met Harkan. Did you change your mind in the city?"

"My experiences weren't that positive," she admitted. "But in this case, he's the reluctant one."

"Borgaz? Really? I saw the way he looked at you that night— like he could devour you."

"Oh, he'll do that all right—all night long if I let him. He just won't do anything else."

"Hmm." Rosie tapped her chin thoughtfully. "I'm not sure it's the same for all of them, but I know with Harkan it wasn't just sex, it was a bond, a claiming. Is that what you want?"

Yes. The immediate response didn't surprise her as much as it should have. Somehow the big, bossy male had worked his way deep into her heart, but she forced herself to shrug casually.

"We agreed that it's just temporary. He only wants to make sure I can manage on my own—which I can, of course."

"Temporary?" Her friend's eyes were far too knowing. "I doubt that's true—for either of you—but I guess you'll have to figure that out yourselves."

She knew she was blushing, but thankfully Rosie changed the subject without waiting for a response. She was telling her how Naffon had scaled the roof of the barn, without any type of harness, when the males returned.

"Why would he do that?" she asked, horrified.

"Because he is a foolish male," Borgaz said, frowning, but he looked more worried than disparaging. "Perhaps I should..."

He looked at her, then shook his head. "He has his own war to fight and it's one he must face alone."

Harkan had immediately gone to Rosie's side, and she did her best to suppress a pang of envy at the easy way he put a possessive arm around her shoulder.

"Are you tired, my mate?"

"Only a little. I enjoyed talking to Mary."

"Next time, Borgaz will bring you to visit us," Harkan said sternly. "So my mate doesn't have to exert herself."

She didn't dare risking a glance at Borgaz as she nodded meekly. "I understand."

"Good. Are you ready to leave, Rosalie?"

Rosie laughed and let him help her to her feet. "All right. I can see you aren't going to stop worrying until we're home again."

She and Borgaz accompanied them to the door. She waved as they left, then snuck a quick glance up at Borgaz. He was frowning, but it was his thoughtful frown, not his annoyed frown.

"Did you have a nice visit with Harkan?"

"It was... informative. He gave me much to consider."

She tilted her head as she studied his face. "About farming?"

"About many things, my curious little fojii."

His frown vanished as he smiled down at her, then he bent his head and kissed her. The kiss felt different somehow, and her heart started to pound as she melted against him. He finally raised his head and smiled again, his eyes glowing.

"We will talk tonight," he promised. "But I want to get as much planted today as possible. Harkan said there will be storms later in the week."

"Okay. I need to hang the laundry out to dry and check on my seedlings."

"Until tonight." He brushed his lips across hers again and headed back to the field, his tail flicking.

Did males talk about things the same way women did? Had Harkan convinced him to stop holding back? It seemed unlikely, but she allowed herself to hope as she went about her chores.

She had just finished hanging up the laundry when she heard another horse. Good grief. Two sets of visitors in one day. She peered around the sheet, then smiled as S'kal dismounted and went to greet him.

"I didn't expect to see you again. I thought the caravan was heading back to Port Cantor."

"It is—we're leaving today. I wanted to stop by and check on you first, little Mary." His eyes were as penetrating as Rosie's and she laughed as she shook her head.

"I'm just fine, thank you. No one needs to worry about me."

"I'm very glad to hear that." He smiled at her. "And in that case, I will merely ask if there is anything you wish me to procure for you from Port Cantor?"

She gave a brief, wistful thought to her mother's necklace but shook her head.

"No—"

"She doesn't need anything from you," Borgaz growled, suddenly appearing in front of her, his tail lashing angrily.

"I hardly think she needs you to speak for her. Especially since we're such old friends."

With a start, she realized S'kal was being deliberately provocative.

"S'kal was just leaving," she said quickly, but both males ignored her.

"You will not return here."

Borgaz's fangs were clearly visible as his lips peeled back from his teeth, but S'kal only raised a mocking brow.

"Again, that's not your decision. It is her land, after all, and you are merely a visitor."

A visitor? He was so much more than that, but before she could decide how to express their relationship, Borgaz prowled closer to S'kal. The two males were of equal height and build and her heart started to thud against her chest.

"I will not allow you to interfere," Borgaz growled.

"You think you can stop me? How amusing."

The menace in the air made her shiver as the two males began to circle each other.

"Stop! What's gotten into the both of you? I think it's time for you to leave, S'kal."

He bowed gracefully. "Of course, little Mary. Whatever *you* wish. But do not forget that I am available if you need assistance—with anything at all."

"She doesn't need your assistance," Borgaz snarled and leaped for his throat.

"Borgaz, no!"

But she was too late. The two males fought savagely, fangs flashing as they grappled. Borgaz managed to knock S'kal to the ground, but S'kal brought him down as well. She darted forward, but they were rolling across the grass, so tangled together that she couldn't get between them. The harsh sounds of their blows made her shudder, but she bit back her protests and ran for the house instead, looking frantically for something, anything, she could use to stop the fight.

Halfway there, she stumbled across the hose she'd been using to water her seedlings and an idea occurred to her. She picked up the hose and dragged it as close as she could to the two fighting males, then turned it on full force. The water from the well was still ice cold, and she smiled with grim satisfaction at the two identical outraged yells before the two males broke apart.

Borgaz glared at her, but S'kal started to laugh.

"A pleasure as always, little Mary." He held up his hands and backed away when Borgaz snarled. "I'm leaving. I can see that your mate has matters well in hand."

Borgaz's tail continued to lash as he watched S'kal mount his horse, raise a hand, and trot away down the road. He continued to watch until the other male was out of sight, then turned and stalked towards her. His wet clothes clung to his big, powerful frame, his muscles taut and his face etched in harsh lines. Her heart was pounding again, but it wasn't fear this time.

"Mine," he growled, and pounced.

CHAPTER 14

Borgaz's blood roared through his veins, still thrumming from the heat of battle. Another male had dared to challenge him for his mate?

A small rational voice tried to remind him that S'kal hadn't challenged him, but it was lost beneath the overwhelming need to claim his female. Her lips parted as he approached and she might have said something, but it was lost beneath his roar as he reached for her. He caught her arms and dragged her up against him, gripping her ass with one hand as he pulled her against his rampant cock. His other hand wrapped around her braid, holding her in place as he lowered his head and captured her mouth with a demanding kiss.

The sweet scent of her arousal filled his head, urging him on as she moaned against his mouth, and he tore at her clothing, determined to remove any barrier between them. Her hands were just as frantic, ripping at his shirt until her bare breasts met his naked chest and they both groaned.

"Need you, fojii," he growled as he ripped off her skirt to reveal bare, beautiful flesh.

She fumbled at his pants, and he took over with an impatient snarl, freeing his erection even as he lifted her into his arms. The slick folds of her cunt surrounded his cock as he pinned her against the wall of the house.

"Yes, please, now," she panted, rocking against him, and his cock jerked, already on the verge of climax.

He clenched his teeth, determined to hold on as his tail came up and teased against the seam of her ass, circling lightly over the small opening there. She gasped, then shuddered and he could feel her body convulsing just from that light contact.

He buried his head against her neck, licking and sucking the sensitive curve. His fangs ached with the need to claim her but some small fraction of control remained beneath the overwhelming need. He managed not to bite her as his hand reached between their bodies and found the swollen bud of her clit, throbbing against his fingers as he stroked over it and her back arched as she came again.

"So pretty when you come, little fojii. Can't wait any more."

"I don't want you to wait," she gasped, still shuddering.

He pressed her back against the wall, using both hands to part her legs as wide as they would go as he positioned her over his cock. Then he slammed into her, sliding in balls deep in a single hard thrust. She cried out, the impossibly tight channel fluttering wildly around him, and he froze.

"Too much?" His voice was a harsh growl, but he managed not to move as he waited for her response.

"More," she moaned, trying to arch up into him, and he obliged, pulling almost completely out then driving in again and again.

"My mate," he growled.

"Yours," she panted and another bolt of lust surged through him.

Her eyes were dazed with pleasure, her cheeks pink, her inner muscles clenching around him with each stroke. He could feel his climax gathering at the base of his spine, and thrust harder as his hands tightened on her ass.

"And who do you belong to?" he demanded.

Her eyes flashed blue fire even as she quivered in his arms.

"No one."

Stubborn to the end. A fierce, delighted grin crossed his face as he wrapped a hand around her braid again.

"Then who does this delicious little cunt belong to?"

"You. Only you," she gasped as she convulsed around him, and he finally let himself go, surging into her with one final deep stroke as he shuddered and climaxed in endless aching pulses, sucking fiercely at her neck as he came and came and came.

When he finally raised his head, he found her staring at him, her eyes shining. His hand was still wrapped around her braid, but his grip gentled as he carefully lifted her off of his cock and put her feet on the ground. He kept his tail curled around her waist, supporting her as she swayed against him.

"Finally," she said, grinning up at him even as her legs trembled.

"Was I too rough?" he asked, his voice hoarse as remorse hit him.

"Not at all. Although it may be a while before I can walk again."

A strange mixture of pride and remorse filled him at her words and he lifted her back into his arms, cradling her against his chest.

"Then I shall carry you wherever you wish to go."

"Why don't we start with the bedroom? Or maybe the bathroom," she added, looking down at the traces of his seed on her thighs, and the combination of emotions intensified.

"Not yet," he growled.

She tilted her head, considering him, then nodded. He carried her into the bedroom instead, placing her gently on the bed, then joining her and pulling her into his arms.

Her hand stroked idly across his chest, both of them silent. Should he feel regret? He couldn't find it in himself to do so, even though he suspected it would come.

"I suppose I should have asked this before, but can you get me pregnant?" she asked suddenly.

His previously drained cock threatened to fill again at the prospect, but he shook his head.

"I eliminated that possibility after the war."

"Permanently?"

Her voice was carefully neutral, but he raised his head to look at her. Was she... disappointed? Or was he projecting his own wishes?

He dipped his hand between her legs and they immediately parted for him. He rubbed his seed into her skin, marking her with his scent, even if it was only temporarily.

"It could be reversed," he finally admitted, and felt her quiver but she didn't respond directly.

"Why now? Was it the fight?"

It had certainly been a factor, but it had been his conversation with Harkan that had actually caused him to reconsider.

"When did you know Rosie was your mate?" he'd asked the other male.

"As soon as I saw her." Harkan had grinned. "Even though I was delirious at the time. I was ill when I arrived—a lingering aftereffect of that cursed war that was slowly killing me."

"But you mated her anyway?"

"How could I not? Even if all we had was a few brief moments of happiness, why not seize them?"

The conversation had moved on to other subjects but the words stayed with him. Perhaps he couldn't stay with Mary forever, but why not share what they could now?

"And are we mated?" There was that neutral voice again, and she wasn't looking at him. "Rosie said that's how it is for some people."

"Not for an Erythran. I did not give you a mating bite to seal the connection," he said quietly, and her eyes flew up to meet his, shadowed with grey.

"Why not?"

"I told you before that I am not a fit mate. I would not bind you to me."

"Or bind yourself?"

He wished he could tell her there was nothing he wanted more, but admitting that wouldn't change anything. He remained silent and she didn't repeat the question.

They lay in silence until he noticed her stomach rumbling.

"You are hungry," he said abruptly, rolling to the side of the bed and lifting her into his arms.

He couldn't make himself a proper mate, but he could take care of her.

"I guess I am," she agreed, smiling up at him. "But you really don't have to carry me everywhere."

"I enjoy it."

She rolled her eyes, but she was still smiling.

"In that case, how about that bath now?"

He wanted to protest, to urge her not to wash away his scent, but he forced himself to nod.

He settled her on the counter while he started the water, then carried her into the shower. Her small body fit neatly against his, her curves a perfect match to his hard planes. He washed her carefully, but her enthusiastic response distracted him, and when he made her come on his hand the sight of her pleasure almost pushed him over the edge again.

"Now food?" he asked, as he rubbed the towel slowly over her body, but she shook her head.

"I'm not in the mood for grilled cheese right now."

"I could make something else."

Her small fingers stroked his cock and he groaned.

"Not now," she said firmly. "Take me back to bed."

"You are not sore?"

"Nope. Bed. Now."

He laughed and carried her back to bed, then spent his time exploring her. He almost made her come with his tongue, but he was greedy and wanted to be inside her for that last delicious little shiver. This time was slower, gentler, and his cock ached as he sank into her welcoming warmth, his eyes on her face as she began to tremble beneath him.

"Give me your tail," she whispered.

She shivered again as his tail slipped between them, the tip caressing the delicate ring, gathering her slickness before pushing in just a tiny bit.

"Do you want more?"

She nodded, biting her lip as she looked up at him, and he slid deeper. The increased fullness made her even tighter around his cock, and he clenched his teeth, trying to hang on as she moved experimentally.

"Am I hurting you?" he asked, his voice rough with the strain of holding back.

"No. It feels... full. Good."

She was panting now, her cheeks pink as she rocked against him, and he started to thrust. He raised her hips, opening her more to his touch and she gave a startled gasp, then started to come, rippling helplessly around him, the tight grip bringing on his own climax as his cock erupted, filling her with his useless seed.

They collapsed onto the bed in a pile of limp limbs, and he stroked her hair back from her damp face.

"How do you feel?"

"Wonderful. Sleepy."

"Not hungry?"

"Not now. Ask me when I wake up."

She drifted into sleep, and once again he found himself watching over her as the day turned to night. He knew the longer he stayed, the harder it would be to leave, but he stayed anyway.

CHAPTER 15

Once again Mary woke up alone, and she sighed. It had been dark when she woke up after her nap the previous afternoon, but she'd persuaded him to let her cook dinner. She'd made a simple frittata with the first of the eggs from her chickens and some of the vegetables that Ferdie had brought her. As they ate, they talked and it was both like and unlike their previous meals.

She didn't bring up any difficult subjects and they talked easily enough, but there was a simmering thread of awareness beneath their conversation. The fact that he was still holding back made her chest ache, but she suspected this was a mountain he would have to climb by himself.

Eventually he carried her back to bed and made love to her so slowly and sweetly that she found herself hoping anyway—but she still woke up alone.

She sighed and got dressed, then had a lonely breakfast before heading outside. Today she was tackling the greenhouse. Most of the plastic panels were still intact, but the inside was a mess and she was determined to clear it out. Borgaz had promised to replace the missing panes, and she found herself looking through the empty frames, searching for that tall red figure.

Dammit. She'd been so determined not to rely on him and now she missed him so much it was like a physical ache. *Don't be ridiculous.* She knew he had other things to attend to in the mornings. *He still could have stayed with me, at least this once,* she thought crossly, yanking on a stubborn dead vine that had wound its way up the wall. It finally pulled free, but as it did it pulled a shelf free as well and it came crashing towards her. She flinched back and then Borgaz was there, pulling her beneath him as the heavy shelf crashed down on his back.

He winced, but his scowl was directed at her, not the shelf, as he lifted her back to her feet.

"Foolish little fojii. Why didn't you wait for me?"

"Because you weren't here," she yelled, fear and frustration driving her. "If you're that worried about me, stop leaving me."

He had the nerve to look surprised.

"You know I promised to help Temel."

"That's fine," she snapped. "But don't lecture me about what I do. I have a farm to get running, with or without your help. And I don't need your help anyway."

"You are angry with me."

"No kidding."

She crossed her arms and glared at him.

"Because of what happened between us?"

He looked so horrified that some of her anger faded.

"Of course not. Well, in a way. I don't like waking up alone, especially after we've been... intimate."

He visibly flinched, more than he had when the shelf hit him.

"It is not a good idea for me to remain with you."

"Why not?"

"I am a... restless sleeper."

The explanation sounded weak to her, but he was clearly troubled by the idea. She sighed, the last of her anger disappearing.

"Couldn't we at least try?"

He hesitated, then slowly dipped his head.

"I will consider it."

Even that seemed torn from him, so she decided to let it drop.

"Are you leaving again?"

"No, I am all yours."

If only that were true. Her heart ached, but she forced a smile.

"In that case, let's see what we can do about getting the greenhouse ready. The seedlings are almost ready for transplanting."

He nodded and they set to work. They usually tackled separate projects, but they quickly fell into an easy rhythm. It was... nice working with him, she decided, but it also made her more conscious of how much she had missed him earlier. If there was any hope for a future between them, she was going to have to get to the bottom of whatever was troubling him.

Her normal instinct would be to confront him and demand answers, but for once she was willing to take a slower approach. The last thing she wanted to do was to cause him pain. With that in mind, she kept the conversation light and focused on their task. By late afternoon, the greenhouse had been readied and the only job that remained was replacing the missing panes. He started on that while she went inside to prepare dinner.

She decided on stuffed cabbage rolls and was just pulling them out of the oven when he joined her.

"Perfect timing," she said cheerfully. "These can rest while you shower."

He gave an unexpected groan and pulled her into his arms. He was still damp from working, the scent of soil mingling with his own spicy scent, but she went willingly.

"Do you know how much I want this?" he demanded, his voice harsh. "Shared work and shared pleasure. A true home."

"I want that too," she admitted, finally facing the truth. "With you."

He kissed her, his mouth equally demanding, then reluctantly let her go.

"I should shower."

"All right." She watched him go, then smiled as an idea occurred to her.

After placing dinner back in the oven to keep warm, she crept quietly into the bathroom. He was still in the shower, and she slipped out of her clothes and went to join him. He looked surprised, then pleased, then shocked as she dropped to her knees in front of him.

"Fojii," he groaned, but his hand was already wrapped around her braid and she hid a smile as she took him in her hands. She'd deliberately left her hair restrained, knowing how much he loved the braid.

"Hush," she whispered, letting her breath wash over his damp cock, and he shuddered.

This was the first time she'd really studied him and she took her time, stroking the thick shaft. It wasn't a single smooth column like that of a human male, but a wide, undulating length. The tip was slightly pointed rather than rounded, and she suspected that made it easier for him to penetrate her, opening her for the thickness that followed. She licked the tip experimentally and he groaned again, his hand tightening in her hair.

The feeling of being restrained made her nipples stiffen and she moved closer, rubbing them against his legs as she took more of him into her mouth. His salty, spicy taste washed over her tongue and it was her turn to moan, sucking eagerly. He was simply too big for her to take more than the first few inches, but she did her best, using her hands to meet her mouth as he guided her strokes.

More hot, delicious liquid filled her mouth and she reached down to cup the heavy weight of his balls. He gave a choked cry and then he was thrusting harder, faster into her mouth as she did her best to take more of him. His balls tightened and he gasped a warning, but she only tightened her grip and sucked harder until he exploded in her mouth. She swallowed as much as she could, but there was so much that some trickled down across her breasts before he finally shuddered to a halt.

With a last gentle lick, she pulled back and smiled up at him. His finger traced the path of his seed down across her breasts and then his expression turned feral. Two seconds later she was bent over the shower bench as he thrust into her from behind, hard and perfect and hers.

Dinner was cold after all, but neither one of them cared. He pulled her onto his lap and fed her bites of food as she snuggled against him.

"I will try," he announced as they finished eating.

"Try what?" she mumbled. Sated from food and sex, she was already half asleep.

"To remain with you."

That brought her head up, searching his face anxiously.

"Are you sure?"

"Sure that I want to try? Yes. Sure that I will succeed? No."

"Thank you for trying," she said quietly.

He nodded and sent her off to bed while he cleaned up the kitchen. No longer sleepy, she was still awake when he joined her a short time later.

"You don't have to do this if you don't want to," she whispered as he tucked her against his side.

"I want to, very much. I just... I hope."

She nodded and stroked his chest, carefully avoiding his scars. Both of them were tense, and it seemed to take a long time before she fell asleep, but she must have done so because she was awakened by a harsh cry. She raised her head and saw his face was contorted, grimacing as if in pain. Whimpers escaped his lips as he tossed his head back and forth on the pillow, gripping the sheets so tightly that they threatened to tear.

She touched his arm gently, keeping her voice soft and soothing.

"Borgaz, you're having a nightmare... Wake up."

He didn't respond. His body tensed even more, and he began to bark incomprehensible words in a language she didn't recognize. But even though she didn't understand the words, the urgency and desperation were clear.

She tried giving him a gentle shake, speaking a little louder but using the same reassuring tone.

"Borgaz! You're here with me, you're safe."

Suddenly his eyes snapped open, but she could tell he didn't see her, just some unknown danger. His breathing came in ragged gasps and sweat beaded on his forehead before he snarled and pounced on top of her. His fangs appeared, his face etched in lines of pain and fear as his hand went to her throat. She made no attempt to escape his grip, still talking to him in a low soothing voice.

"You're with me, you're safe."

Her words finally seemed to get through to him, and his grip gradually eased as his eyes cleared, but then he realized he was pinning her to the mattress and jerked away as if scalded, scrambling to the far side of the bed.

She didn't try to follow, giving him his space as she spoke calmly.

"You were dreaming. I think about the war. You're with me now, you're safe. Whatever happened, it's over now."

"Can't you see? It's never over. I knew this was a mistake."

His voice was a tortured cry, and then he was gone, fleeing the room as she stared after him. So this was why he didn't want to share her bed. She hesitated, trying to decide if she should let him have time to think, then shook her head decisively. To hell with that.

She pulled on her nightgown and robe and padded silently through the house and out towards the barn. If he was still there, if he cared enough to remain and watch over her, she thought there was still hope. If he had also fled the barn... Well, she'd face that if it had happened.

Her heart pounded as she slipped through the now silent doors, then sighed with relief. He was still there, crouched against the far wall, his face drawn.

"Please leave," he said roughly, without looking up.

"No."

For a second his expression changed, a brief softening before turning harsh again.

"Stubborn little fojii."

"You're damn right. And in case you've forgotten, this is my barn. Although I hoped it would become our barn," she added softly, and he shuddered.

"And now you know why it could not."

"Why not? Because you had a nightmare?"

His laugh held no humor.

"Nightmare? It is far worse than that. I could have hurt you."

"But you didn't."

Her words didn't seem to penetrate. He only shook his head.

"I refuse to take that chance."

"And what gives you the right to make that decision?" she snapped. "This involves me as well."

For a second she thought she might have reached him, but then he shook his head again and she sighed. This wasn't getting them anywhere. She went and sat down next to him. He jumped and she thought he might leave, but he remained next to her.

"Tell me about it," she said quietly.

He was silent for a long time, but she waited patiently and he finally began to speak.

"I didn't have a choice about joining the military, but I liked it. I liked being part of a unit, or being useful, of training my body and my mind."

Another long pause.

"And then we were sent to Vizal. Even that wasn't bad at first, more like war games than actual combat. But then people started to die and it became all too real. I saw things... I did things..."

He shuddered.

"And it went on and on until I turned into someone I didn't even recognize. For months after the war ended, I would look at myself in the mirror and see a stranger. I'm not sure how long I would have lasted if it hadn't been for Temel. He refused to give up on me, on any of us—which is why we ended up here. He should have known better. It's too late for me."

Up until then she'd remained silent, but she couldn't let that go.

"Don't be stupid."

"Stupid?"

He turned to look at her, his face shocked. At least shock was better than that frozen, harrowed expression.

"Yes, stupid. If I'd thought it was too late to change, I'd still be stuck in Port Cantor. Instead, I'm here, with you."

"I should leave," he muttered.

"And leave me defenseless and alone?"

She widened her eyes innocently when he gave her a suspicious look, and he almost smiled before he shook his head.

"Most females are terrified of my night terrors."

She poked him, hard, with her finger.

"I don't want to hear about any other females. And I'm not like them."

"You most certainly are not. My stubborn little fojii."

"Your cold fojii."

She gave an exaggerated shiver and climbed onto his lap. He tensed and she half-expected him to reject her, but instead his arms closed around her and she settled down in his arms.

"I'm staying right here until the sun rises," she warned him and he made a choked sound that could have been a laugh.

"You would be more comfortable in the house."

"I'm more comfortable with you."

She took a firm grip on his shirt, then let herself relax. She actually slept a little, although she didn't think he did, but he kept his arms around her, and when the sun rose they were still together.

CHAPTER 16

*L*ater that morning, Borgaz rode slowly towards the main house. After Mary woke in his arms in the barn, she'd insisted that they have breakfast together. He hadn't been able to refuse, even though he had little appetite. His brain had been churning all night, and by the time he pushed his almost untouched plate aside, he'd come up with an idea.

"I need to go and see Temel this morning."

"That's fine." She yawned and gave him a sleepy smile. "I think I'm going to spend a quiet morning sewing. It's about time I started repairing those curtains. That is..." Her smile vanished as she studied his face. "You are coming back, aren't you? You wouldn't leave me without saying anything?"

"Never," he promised, and her smile returned.

He'd kissed her and set off but Arros slowed as they approached the house, clearly picking up on his uncertainty. Fortunately, he spotted Temel in the orchard before he reached it and he swung down, then set Arros loose to graze. Temel didn't look up as he approached, still focused on the notes he was taking.

"My research says these trees should be pruned to be more productive, but they are good healthy stock."

Healthy stock. Would he ever be healthy, or was he permanently damaged? It was a shame he couldn't prune away his damaged parts.

When he didn't respond, Temel looked up, then quietly put his datapad to one side.

"What is it?"

"I want to claim Mary as my mate," he burst out, but Temel only raised an eyebrow.

"I thought that was obvious from the moment I saw the two of you together. Is there a problem?"

"You know I have... problems sleeping?"

"I do. Have you told her?"

"She experienced it for herself. I woke last night to find myself on top of her, my hand on her neck. I thought she was an enemy."

Temel's gaze was intent on his face.

"Did you hurt her?"

"No, but what if I had?"

After a brief hesitation, Temel started walking across the orchard and Borgaz followed him.

"I was there in the hospital when you woke," Temel said softly as they reached the stone wall surrounding the trees and looked out across the pastures. "You did the same thing, crouching over a nurse and snarling at anyone who approached."

His heart sank as he shook his head.

"I don't remember that."

"I didn't think you did. But that was right after we retrieved you from the prison camp and you were still half-starved and ill."

"Did I hurt the nurse?" he asked, dread threatening to close his throat.

"No. You undoubtedly scared him, but you didn't damage him at all. And that was when you were most vulnerable. Have you ever hurt anyone?"

He thought back to those earlier times, then shook his head. Scared, yes, but never injured.

"Then why do you think you'd hurt your mate?"

Rationally, the words made sense, but emotionally, he was still afraid.

"I don't even want to scare her."

"Was she scared?"

Was she? She certainly hadn't shown any signs of fear, he remembered, even tracking him down and refusing to leave. His lips curved in a reluctant smile.

"I'm not sure she's afraid of anything."

"Then concentrate on that. I brought all of you here for a chance to make a new start and I think you can, with her. If she is willing to accept you as you are, why not take that gift instead of making both of you unhappy?"

His friend's words were an uncomfortable reminder of her question the previous night—why should he decide for her?

"Perhaps you are right. If she's truly willing to accept me..."

His lips curved again as he imagined a future with his little fojii.

"Then I suggest you go and ask her," Temel said firmly.

He nodded and started to turn away, then looked back.

"And what about you? You said you brought us here to make a new start, but you didn't say anything about a new start yourself."

Temel shrugged, but not before Borgaz saw a flash of sorrow cross his face.

"I have no need for it. As long as my warriors are happy, I will be content."

"Maybe you need a little happiness yourself," he suggested, but Temel only shrugged again and he decided not to pursue it.

Instead, he saluted and went to retrieve Arros. He headed home much more quickly than he'd left, but he was only halfway there when thunder boomed overhead like the cannons from the battlefield and the sky darkened. He flinched, fighting to avoid being thrown back into the past. He considered taking shelter and waiting it out, but dark clouds were already boiling over the horizon, rapidly approaching their farm.

Fuck. He couldn't leave Mary to face that alone. He urged Arros into a gallop as the thunder echoed across the valley again. Shadowy images of war and destruction danced in front of his eyes, but his mate was more important than his past. The rain struck, pouring down like bullets, but he kept going, determined to make it home.

CHAPTER 17

Even though Mary had urged Borgaz to go, she still found herself staring out the window as she sewed and listening for the sound of hoofbeats. She knew he was still troubled, but at least now she understood why. *And maybe I can help him.* As long as he didn't give up, neither would she.

The morning turned unusually quiet, the air thick with humidity, and she shivered, suddenly uneasy. Putting aside her sewing, she paced to the back porch and looked outside. The air had an odd yellowish tinge, and her heart skipped a beat as she recognized the signs of an upcoming storm. They didn't happen often but they tended to hit hard and fast, and she could already see darkness on the horizon.

Fuck. She cast a worried glance in the direction Borgaz had ridden, then set to work. Herding the chickens into their nesting boxes and locking them down took longer than she had hoped, and the first drops of rain hit as she ran for the field where her cow and calf were grazing. Fortunately, they were already at the barn door and she was able to get them inside before the real rain hit.

By the time she stepped back outside, it was coming down in sheets, plastering her hair to her head and making it difficult to see. A faint banging sounded over the wind, and she realized the greenhouse door was open. Determined not to waste their hard work, she fought against the winds as she made her way over to the door and somewhat managed to get it closed and fastened.

The house wasn't far, but lightning struck a nearby tree just as she started to return. The deafening crack split the air, the shock sending her flying forward into the mud. Her vision dimmed as she struggled to draw breath, but she finally managed to raise her head, blinking at the ruined tree through the heavy curtain of rain. The ankle she'd injured before was throbbing again, but it supported her weight as she lurched to her feet and headed for the house again.

The wind had changed direction, trying to force her off her feet as she struggled through the mud towards the house, and then Borgaz was there, his big body bent against the wind as he reached her and pulled her into the safety of his arms. Together they fought their way back to the house. The wind threatened to tear the door from his hands, but he finally managed to wrestle it closed and the noise of the storm abated enough for her to hear herself think.

She shuddered, unable to stop shivering and he wrapped his arms around her, holding her tightly. He flinched as thunder boomed again, but his grip on her never loosened. Her body finally stopped shaking and she managed to raise her head and smile up at him.

"I've never been so glad to see anyone in my life."

His face was unusually pale and drawn, but he returned her smile.

"You should have remained in the house, but somehow I didn't think you would."

"I had to make sure the animals were safe."

"I saw when I stabled Arros. I'm sorry I wasn't here to help."

"You were here when it counted," she said softly. "I told you I could manage on my own—and I could—but Rosie was right, it's better to share it with someone."

Amber eyes glowed at her.

"Even a bossy, damaged warrior?"

Her throat threatened to close, but she nodded firmly.

"Especially a bossy, damaged warrior."

A cold drop of rain dripped down her neck. She shivered again, and he frowned.

"Go and get out of those wet clothes," he ordered. "I'll build a fire."

"Definitely bossy," she teased, and he shook his head, then turned her towards the bedroom and sent her on her way with a quick smack on her ass.

This time her shiver was not due to cold, but he was right—she needed to dry off. By the time she'd wrapped herself in a warm robe and toweled her hair as dry as possible, the fire was roaring. He'd removed his wet shirt and replaced his soaked jeans with a pair of loose sleeping pants.

By unspoken agreement, they sat on the rug in front of the fire, staring into the crackling flames as the storm raged outside. His arm was wrapped around her shoulders as she leaned against him, half-asleep after the interrupted night and the fight against the weather.

"Did you mean it?" he asked finally, his voice low. "About sharing your life with me?"

She looked up at his face, infinitely strange and beloved in the flickering light, and smiled.

"Of course I did. I love you, Borgaz."

He shuddered, tension leaching out of his muscles.

"And my night terrors truly do not disturb you?"

"They only disturb me because they cause you pain. I'm not frightened of them, nor of you."

His eyes closed as he muttered a brief, thankful prayer.

"I love you too, my fojii, and I wish to claim you as my mate. Do you accept my claim?"

Instead of answering him in words, she brushed her hair away from her neck, exposing the spot he spent so much time kissing. His eyes glowed, but instead of biting her immediately, he only stroked a finger over the rapidly throbbing pulse.

"I must prepare you first."

"Prepare me?" The words sounded rather ominous, and her heart skipped a beat. "What does that mean?"

"You'll see." He suddenly grinned, looking lighter than she'd ever seen him. "Don't worry, fojii, you'll enjoy it."

Since preparing her consisted of removing her clothes and kissing every inch of her body, he was right, she did enjoy it. So much so that she was tugging impatiently on his horns before he groaned and pulled back long enough to strip off his pants. His body gleamed in the firelight and her mouth went dry. His cock looked even bigger than usual, a glistening drop of precum beading on the tip. She couldn't resist reaching for it, swiping her thumb over it before sliding her hand down the thick shaft. He hissed a breath, then caught her hand and drew it gently away, kissing her palm.

"This is usually done from behind, but I wish to see your face."

"All right," she whispered.

She expected him to lay her down on the rug, but instead he lifted her onto his lap, holding her suspended over his cock.

"Hold on to me," he urged and she gripped his shoulders.

As soon as she did, he lowered her over his cock as he thrust up into her, filling her in a single deep stroke, and she cried out at the exquisite mixture of pleasure and a delicious stretching burn.

"Too much?" His voice was a harsh growl, but she was already trying to move against him.

His hands dropped to her ass, holding her tightly in place as he began to pump into her, lowering her over him with each thrust, each rough slide of his cock sending shockwaves of pleasure through her body.

"More," she demanded.

He obeyed, fucking her hard and fast, his undulating cock dragging over each sensitive spot with every thrust. The delicious pressure built again, and her breath caught in her throat as she grabbed his horns and held on. The rhythm of his hips became wilder, pounding into her until he roared and buried his face in her neck. A sudden sharp sting was followed by drugging waves of pleasure as another orgasm shuddered through her and his seed jetted into her in hot, seemingly endless bursts.

All she could do was cling to him as her body slowly stopped quivering. He gave her neck a last gentle lick and raised his head to smile at her.

"My mate."

He said it with such pride and happiness that unexpected tears sprang to her eyes, and he gave her a worried look.

"Was that too much?"

"You don't need to keep asking me that," she muttered. "If I don't like something, you'll know."

His face relaxed again as he grinned.

"I'm sure I will. I certainly hope you liked it because I intend to do it again."

She gasped as his cock started to swell inside her.

"Already?"

"Yes. But this time the traditional way."

He lifted her free and gently placed her on her hands and knees in front of him before notching his cock at her entrance. His tail came up to tease her ass, and she wiggled happily.

"Ready?" he asked, stroking his hand down her back.

"Of course I'm—"

Her ability to speak vanished as he drove hard and deep, and she gave herself over to pleasure.

THE NEXT MORNING SHE SMILED HAPPILY WHEN SHE WOKE to find him wrapped around her. His night terrors hadn't disturbed their sleep, but considering how often and how enthusiastically he'd made love to her, perhaps he was simply too exhausted. *Not a bad solution*, she thought with another smile, keeping him too exhausted from sex to have nightmares.

A big hand curved around her waist, then up to pluck at a still swollen nipple.

"Good morning, my mate."

"Good morning," she echoed, rolling over to face him. The storm had passed, and the morning light shone on his horns and his gleaming red skin. He had the wicked grin on his face and she returned it. "You're looking particularly devilish this morning. Why?"

"I'm simply happy."

"Me too."

She reached for him, but he laughed and slipped away.

"Hold that thought for just a moment. I want to call up to the main house and make sure they came through the storm unscathed."

He picked up his comm and held a brief, muttered conversation before frowning as he came back to the bed.

"Is something wrong?"

"I hope not. We had reports that a small group of travelers were headed in this direction. Temel went to find them and make sure they're all right." He shook his head, smiling faintly. "His first instinct is always to care for others. He needs to care for himself as well."

"Do you want to go and check on him?" she asked reluctantly, but he shook his head.

"No. If he needs me, he'll call. This is where I want to be."

"Good, then come back to bed."

"I will, but first." He dropped down on his knees next to the bed and her heart started to pound. "As an Erythran, the mating bite marks you as mine, but I want it all. Will you marry me?"

"I thought you didn't believe in human marriage," she said, choking back a sob.

"I believe in it with you. Will you marry me, my fojii?"

"Of course I will."

She launched herself into his arms, blinded by tears but knowing that he would catch her, that he would always catch her. Her beloved, bossy mate.

EPILOGUE

Ten months later...

"Never again," Borgaz swore, pacing back and forth across the bedroom floor. "You are never having another child in the middle of winter. What if the snow had been too heavy for Drakkar to make it? What if we'd been trapped here?"

"But he did make it and we weren't trapped," Mary said calmly as she nursed their beautiful new daughter. They had named her Virginia Mae after both their mothers, and her skin was a perfect pale pink beneath a tiny mop of dark hair. "And talking about the next child when a woman has just been through labor is probably not the best timing."

He swore again and returned to the bed, putting his arm around her.

"I'm sorry, my little fojii. I found the situation... difficult."

"You should have tried it from this end," she said dryly, then nudged his arm sympathetically.

While it wasn't the same as being in labor, she did understand how difficult he found it to be in a situation he couldn't control. She'd half-expected him to start ordering her not to be in pain.

He sighed, and finally relaxed as he stroked their daughter's cheek.

"But she is worth it, is she not?"

"Definitely. Aren't you glad you had the procedure reversed?"

Even though he admitted he wanted a child, he'd hesitated. At first he'd wanted to wait until everything on the farm was running to his satisfaction, but she'd gently reminded him that there would always be work to be done.

She knew he also worried about his night terrors, but although they had not completely vanished, they had eased considerably after their mating, and a month after they were married he decided he was ready. Just like Rosie, she suspected she'd become pregnant on their first try—although that hadn't stopped him from repeating his efforts with great enthusiasm.

She smiled as he leaned closer and brushed a kiss to her mating mark. In spite of her exhaustion and the lingering soreness between her legs, excitement shivered through her before she gave him a mock frown.

"Stop that. Drakkar said we had to wait for at least a month."

"Yes, fojii." His eyes dropped to her breast as she gently removed their now sleeping daughter, and they glowed amber. "But perhaps I can find other ways of pleasuring you."

"And I may be willing to let you try. In a week. Or possibly two."

He laughed and pressed a quick kiss to her lips.

"I will wait for you to let me know. Should I put Virginia Mae in her basket?"

She yawned and gave a sleepy nod.

"Yes, then come and hold me."

He put the baby down, but instead of returning immediately to the bed, he hesitated next to it.

"I have something for you."

He cleared his throat, looking oddly nervous, then pulled out a long sparkling strand. She stared at it in disbelief as she recognized the familiar jewelry.

"Is… is that my mother's necklace?"

"Yes. S'kal still has connections in the city, and he had them hunt it down."

"You asked S'kal for help?"

The two of them had reached a truce, but they would never be the best of friends. He only shrugged.

"I wanted you to have it."

"But it must have cost so many credits."

He shrugged again.

"I told you I had little time to spend my pay during the war, and little desire to do so afterwards. This I desired. May I put it on you?"

She nodded, still stunned, and he fastened the necklace around her throat, a cool, familiar weight. She traced it with her fingers, then gave him a watery smile.

"One day this will belong to Virginia Mae. I pray she's never desperate enough to sell it, but if she has to, I hope it leads her to a mate as perfect as you."

His smile looked a little shaky as well as he drew her close.

"Perfect, eh? I will have to remind you that you said that."

"Well, maybe not perfect," she began, and he laughed. "But perfect for me. I love you, Borgaz."

"I love you too, my little fojii, and I know you are perfect for me."

She snuggled against him, and as her eyes closed, she touched the necklace, imagining her mother smiling down at her, and went happily to sleep.

AUTHOR'S NOTE

Thank you so much for reading **Borgaz**! It's so much fun to be back in the Seven Brides world with a new set of warriors! I hope you enjoyed my grumpy warrior and his determined heroine as much as I enjoyed writing them!

Whether you enjoyed the story or not, it would mean the world to me if you left an honest review on Amazon – reviews are one of the best ways to help other readers find my books!

As usual, I have to thank my readers for coming on these adventures with me - I couldn't do it without you!

And, as always, a special thanks to my beta team – Janet S, Nancy V, and Kitty S. Your thoughts and comments are incredibly helpful!

Up next!

AUTHOR'S NOTE

How the Aliens Were Won
continues with Temel!

Temel has always been more concerned for his warriors than for himself, giving up on any hope of love and family long ago. Then he meets a female who arouses all of the feelings he never thought to have.

But he has his warriors to protect and she has responsibilities of her own - how can he ask her to take a chance on a warrior who has nothing left to offer except his devotion?

Temel is available on Amazon!

And if you'd like to read about more about how the farm became available, check out ***You Got Alien Trouble!*** - Rosie and Harkan's story!

You Got Alien Trouble! is available on Amazon!

To make sure you don't miss out on any new releases, please visit my website and sign up for my newsletter!

www.honeyphillips.com

OTHER TITLES

HOMESTEAD WORLDS

Seven Brides for Seven Alien Brothers

Artek

Benjar

Callum

Drakkar

Endark

Frantor

Gilmat

You Got Alien Trouble!

How the Aliens Were Won

Borgaz

Temel

Cosmic Fairy Tales

Jackie and the Giant

Blind Date with an Alien

Her Alien Farmhand

Cyborgs on Mars

High Plains Cyborg

The Good, the Bad, and the Cyborg

A Fistful of Cyborg

A Few Cyborgs More

The Magnificent Cyborg

The Outlaw Cyborg

The Cyborg with No Name

Cyborg Rider

KAISARIAN EMPIRE

The Alien Abduction Series

Anna and the Alien

Beth and the Barbarian

Cam and the Conqueror

Deb and the Demon

Ella and the Emperor

Faith and the Fighter

Greta and the Gargoyle

Hanna and the Hitman

Izzie and the Icebeast

Joan and the Juggernaut

Kate and the Kraken

Lily and the Lion

Mary and the Minotaur
Nancy and the Naga
Olivia and the Orc
Pandora and the Prisoner
Quinn and the Queller
Rita and the Raider
Sara and the Spymaster
Tammy and the Traitor

Folsom Planet Blues
Alien Most Wanted: Caged Beast
Alien Most Wanted: Prison Mate
Alien Most Wanted: Mastermind
Alien Most Wanted: Unchained

Stranded with an Alien
Sinta - A SciFi Holiday Tail

Cosmic Cinema
My Fair Alien
Skruj

Horned Holidays

Krampus and the Crone

A Gift for Nicholas

A Kiss of Frost

Treasured by the Alien

Mama and the Alien Warrior

A Son for the Alien Warrior

Daughter of the Alien Warrior

A Family for the Alien Warrior

The Nanny and the Alien Warrior

A Home for the Alien Warrior

A Gift for the Alien Warrior

A Treasure for the Alien Warrior

Three Babies and the Alien Warrior

Sanctuary for the Alien Warrior

Exposed to the Elements

The Naked Alien

The Bare Essentials

A Nude Attitude

The Buff Beast

The Strip Down

The Alien Invasion Series

Alien Selection

Alien Conquest

Alien Prisoner

Alien Breeder

Alien Alliance

Alien Hope

Alien Castaway

Alien Chief

Alien Ruler

COZY MONSTERS

Fairhaven Falls

Cupcakes for My Orc Enemy

Trouble for My Troll

Fireworks for My Dragon Boss

The Single Mom and the Orc

Mistletoe for My Minotaur

Monster Between the Sheets

Extra Virgin Gargoyle

Without a Stitch

The Five Kingdoms

The Orc's Hidden Bride

The Orc's Stolen Bride

ABOUT THE AUTHOR

Honey Phillips writes steamy science fiction stories about hot alien warriors and the human women they can't resist. From abductions to invasions, the ride might be rough, but the end always satisfies.

Honey wrote and illustrated her first book at the tender age of five. Her writing has improved since then. Her drawing skills, unfortunately, have not. She loves writing, reading, traveling, cooking, and drinking champagne - not necessarily in that order.

Honey loves to hear from her wonderful readers! You can stalk her at any of the following locations...

www.facebook.com/HoneyPhillipsAuthor
www.bookbub.com/authors/honey-phillips
www.instagram.com/HoneyPhillipsAuthor
www.honeyphillips.com